Last Bite

"The gila usually picks on smaller prey," Farrow said nonchalantly as he set down the cage, "but this poor fella didn't eat last night, so who knows?"

Jaw clenched against the burning pain in his shoulder, Blancanales looked down at the caged beast pacing within its confines. The creature, perhaps drawn by the scent of fresh blood, turned its head upward so that it was looking back at Pol. Blancanales had looked Death in the face before and had always managed to walk away, but this time he doubted that he'd be so fortunate. Still, if he was going to die, he was determined that he'd go out the same way he lived, in control, a smile on his face.

"Well, gila darlin'," he cooed to the beast, "save the last dance for me...."

"Able Team will go anywhere, do anything, in order to complete their mission."
—*West Coast Review of Books*

Mack Bolan's

ABLE TEAM.

ABLE TEAM.
Blood Mark

Dick Stivers

A GOLD EAGLE BOOK FROM
WORLDWIDE.

TORONTO • NEW YORK • LONDON • PARIS
AMSTERDAM • STOCKHOLM • HAMBURG
ATHENS • MILAN • TOKYO • SYDNEY

First edition February 1989

ISBN 0-373-61240-0

Special thanks and acknowledgment to
Ron Renauld for his contribution to this work.

Printed in U.S.A.

PROLOGUE

At night from a distance, Las Vegas looks like a giant light bulb screwed into the barren desert floor, luring tourists, mothlike, to the dazzling brilliance of its legendary Strip and downtown casinos. Many of those who heed its call suffer fates not unlike those experienced by fluttery-winged creatures who dare to venture too close to the source of illumination. Few people roll into the mesmerizing city without dreams of striking a quick fortune; most slink away in retreat soon after, somewhat wiser and considerably poorer. By its very nature, Vegas is a hard town—brutal to the vulnerable, self-destructive to the compulsive and fatal to those who make no concession to the different rules that govern those pockets of concentrated avarice and glandular gratification.

Las Vegas should have been the last place an ex-con looking to go straight would head, and yet as soon as twenty-year-old Billy Hobbs was released from the state pen in Carson City, he boarded an Amtrak train and rode it south to that granddaddy of gambling resorts west of the Rockies. But it wasn't the action centering around the casinos that had prompted his move. The stipulations of his parole required that he be entrusted to the care of his uncle, Vincent Hobbs, until he reached the age of twenty-one. Hobbs worked for the *Las Vegas Herald* and lived in a modest house trailer off East Fremont, near the Oran K. Gragson Highway. The spot was reasonably removed from the glitter.

Anxious to put his life back together and to steer clear of any digressions that might lead him to violate his parole, Billy threw himself into work. His uncle got him a job delivering the morning edition of the *Herald*, and on Saturday nights he helped stuff advertising supplements into the Sunday edition. The job was all right for now, but the young man wanted something better, and he started skimming the classifieds daily in hopes of finding a full-time job with a decent wage. There had been several promising listings, but he'd gotten only as far as filling out an application. He was certain that the stigma of his prison sentence was the reason why he'd yet to find work on his own.

But tonight, perhaps, that was all going to change.

Billy hummed to himself, half out of nervousness and half out of excitement, as he drove his uncle's '79 Chevette onto the highway and eased down the accelerator so he could merge with other traffic looping around the outskirts of town. It was after nine, so there were few commuters on the road and he was able to make good time. Billy thought he should show up early for this job interview. He could park and relax a few minutes, psych himself up, make this one count. He'd just showered and shaved and put on his cleanest work clothes, wanting to make as good an impression as possible when he met the man who had called him only two hours ago with a job offer at the company's warehouse near the downtown train yards. Mr. Minkler had told Billy that he was foreman on the graveyard shift at the warehouse and that he might have an opening for a stock boy. As Minkler had explained it, his wife worked for the state Department of Corrections and had come across Billy's file during a routine check for recent parolees who seemed to deserve help making their way back into society. Billy fit the profile and, Minkler said, if he presented himself favorably at the interview, he could begin work as early as the following Monday.

"Yeah!" Billy murmured to himself as he exited the freeway at Las Vegas Boulevard. A nice forty-hour workweek would give him a chance to build up a nest egg by his birthday. As much as he liked his uncle, Billy still longed for the independence that a place of his own would give him. Once he'd found himself a reasonably priced apartment close to work, he calculated that he would stick around Vegas for a year or so to save enough money to allow him to finally move to Los Angeles. Billy figured he could really start a new life for himself there.

Las Vegas Boulevard was just blocks away from the downtown casinos, and Billy deliberately headed north to avoid those beckoning lights. He'd already learned the lesson of temptation. The hard way.

Three years ago he and a few of his high school buddies had gotten drunk up in Reno and had somehow managed to pass for adults when they hit the casinos. He'd taken all the money out of his savings account, all three hundred dollars, thinking that a few hours of gambling would bump up the total to at least four figures. His buddies had even more money, but it had only taken them an hour and a half before they had lost it all. Billy had been suckered by the same gambling fever that had broken his parents' marriage back when he was in grade school. Still drunk, the teenagers had taken their misery out to the parking lot where, at the suggestion of the group's leader, they had hidden in the shadows until they spotted a wealthy couple leaving the casino. Although he'd had his reservations, Billy had played along, still drinking the booze they had with them, and when they'd overpowered the couple in hopes of getting their hands on some money and the keys to a car, Billy was in the thick of it. When the casino security people had intervened, Billy had fought back, cracking one guard's skull with a bottle before he was subdued. The guard survived and provided the most damning testimony in the subsequent trial that had led to the imprisonment of Billy and his three would-be friends. Billy was the first to get out on parole, and he was determined to make damn sure he wouldn't be the first to end up back behind bars. In the three weeks he'd been living with his uncle, Billy had yet to venture within hearing distance of a casino slot machine, much less play one, and he wasn't about to change now.

Just north of downtown was Bonanza Road, an inappropriately named strip that, along with the train tracks, served as the line between the haves and have-nots of Las Vegas. At this late hour Billy saw the most downtrodden of the town's citizenry, some of them loitering near the Rescue Mission, others in front of a windowless liquor store just down the block. Most of them were men, wearing the multilayered soiled apparel of the homeless, their faces stubbled and ruddy from the effects of foul weather and too much drink, their eyes locked in an expression of hopeless desperation.

Billy tried to keep his gaze fixed on the road, but he couldn't help but see the men and feel that wary sense of shame that more fortunate souls are troubled by if they have so much as a shred of conscience or compassion. Billy knew that he could easily have ended up like these other men when he got out of prison. It was only his uncle's dedication and guiding hand that had helped to steer him through his jail term so that he emerged from the experience with a desire to overcome the obstacle it represented.

I won't fail you, Uncle Vinnie, Billy vowed to himself as he continued down the road, crossing under the Union Pacific bridge and making his way to the industrial section of town, which thrived off the rails linking Vegas with the rest of the world. Nondescript cinder-block complexes were spaced in rows along cramped side streets, bathed in the soft, yellowish glow of halogen lamps that contrasted sharply with the harsher glare of neon and incandescent bulbs encrusting the casinos on the other side of the tracks.

Global Imports was tucked away in the back of one of the older industrial complexes, but was easily located by a garage-sized globe that was mounted on the roof and illuminated by a bank of spotlights. Billy parked along the street half a block away, checked the dashboard clock and noted that he was, as expected, nearly ten minutes early. He spent half that extra time inside the Chevette, eyeing himself in the rearview mirror as he practiced his responses to anticipated interview questions. His adolescence behind him, Billy's voice had deepened to the point where he sounded older than his age, and he planned to use that to his advantage. Similarly, his full mustache and trimmed sideburns gave him a further illusion of maturity. Inside, though, he felt as terrified as he had when he was a small child being placed in his first foster home after the suicide of his mother and the failure of the welfare people to locate his father, who had walked out of the picture several years before.

Finally it was time to show up for the interview. Mr. Minkler had instructed Billy to use the back entrance, near the loading docks. As he crossed the parking lot, Billy drew in a deep breath, trying to chase away the butterflies in his stomach.

"Cool, calm, collected," he whispered to himself, recalling his uncle's advice. Just be cool, calm and collected and the rest will be easy.

As he was about to reach the dock area, Billy heard a siren scream to life in the night. It was only a few blocks away. He was startled by the sudden outburst, but he forgot it seconds later when he saw someone lying on the asphalt near a Dumpster next to the back staircase.

Horrified, Billy took a hesitant step toward the figure. In the dim light he could see that it was a man in a uniform and that he wasn't moving.

The sirens were drawing closer.

Billy saw blood pooling near the fallen man's head, and as he drew closer he saw the gore where a bullet had shattered much of the man's skull.

Recoiling, Billy's foot inadvertently kicked something to one side. He glanced down and let out a gasp.

It was a gun.

And not just any gun. Even in the dim light, he knew at once that it was the same handgun that his uncle had reported missing two days after Billy had moved in with him. Vinnie hadn't accused Billy, but the coincidence had been disturbing even then.

Now Billy knew there had been no coincidence. He also knew that the siren drawing closer belonged to a police car responding to a call for help at the warehouse.

"Framed," Billy whispered hoarsely as the situation made itself clear in his mind. He thought he was going to be sick. "I've been framed."

Over his shoulder, Billy saw the blinking light of a police cruiser barreling around the corner and heading for the warehouse. Acting on instinct, Billy grabbed the gun and ran in the opposite direction. He bolted over a short fence and ran full stride across a barren stretch of land between the industrial park and the tracks. When he heard a voice shouting through a bullhorn for him to stop, he whirled around and swung the gun into firing position. The hammer clicked down on an empty chamber. The gun's ammo had been spent.

The dirt around him flew as .357 Magnum slugs pounded into it.

Billy threw aside the gun and once again began to run. He had no idea where he was going. The only thing he knew for sure was that there was no way he was going to go back to prison. He'd die first.

1

The night after Billy Hobbs was framed at Global Imports, a Pizza Monger delivery car with painted pepperonis and other choice toppings adorning its sides, turned into the main driveway serving Fremont Trailer Home Park. The gum-smacking teenager behind the wheel slowed the car as he checked the neat rows of trailers for an address to match the one on his delivery order. The car was fragrant with the warm, tantalizing aroma of the Monger Maniac's Delight, a fourteen-inch pizza smothered with virtually every imaginable ingredient, which was nestled within its cardboard box inside the car's back seat heating unit.

"One-twelve...one-fourteen...one-sixteen," the youth muttered to himself as he read off the posted addresses. His name was Barry. His delivery was for trailer one-eighty, and by the time he'd reached that section of the park, he was having a hard time inching his car through the pedestrian traffic crowding the roadway. The people were all headed in the same direction, toward one of the distant trailers. Impatient at falling behind schedule, Barry punched his horn several times to get people out of his way. Finally he opened his window and called out, "Like, what's going on around here?"

One of the park tenants, a grizzled-looking woman in her seventies, squinted through her bifocals at the driver and yelled, "It's them Yanderses! They're at it again!"

"Yanderses, Yanderses," the teen muttered to himself as he checked his delivery order. "Shit."

"Watch your language, sonny."

"Sorry, ma'am. Those Yanderses, do they live at trailer one-eighty?"

"That's right," the old woman snapped. "And stop honking that horn!"

Barry rolled up his window and swore again as he coaxed the pizzamobile closer to his destination. One-eighty turned out to be at the end of the road, one of three trailers facing a cul-de-sac now filled with spectators gaping at the commotion in front of the Yanders place. When Barry shifted into park and got out to stand for a better look, he made a sour face. This was one pizza that wasn't going to be delivered to the right party.

Standing on the front porch of the trailer was a man well over six feet tall and at least 250 pounds. He wore disheveled clothes and his eyes were lit with the sparkle of someone whose twisted logic had led him to a false sense of self-righteousness. He carried an ax and Barry suspected that somehow the man didn't figure to use it to slice his pizza.

"Bitch!" Dick Yanders howled at his wife, Leila, a frail-looking woman half the man's size and age. She was bound by the wrists to the porch railing, and although she tried to cower away from her husband, there was little she could do to avoid him. She was crying hysterically and wore a look of absolute terror.

"Divorce, huh?" Yanders railed, tightening his grip on the ax. "You want half of everything, huh? Okay, fine. Let's start with the trailer!" Yanders drew back the ax, then swung forward with all his might, slamming the sharp wedge into the aluminum siding.

"Nooooooo!" Leila screamed, staring at the cloven gash in the trailer. "Stop!"

"I just started!" Yanders countered, swinging the ax once more.

Although at least two dozen people were gathered about the cul-de-sac, none of whom tried to intervene in the domestic dispute, including Barry, who ducked back inside his car long enough to haul out the boxed pizza. Standing back in full view of the crowd, he pried the lid open slightly, before calling out, "What am I bid for this delicious pizza?" To his surprise, a handful of arms shot into the air around him and he heard offers ranging between two and five dollars.

As Barry tried to increase the price, another man made his way through the crowd until he was on the front walk leading up to the Yanders trailer. Vincent Hobbs was in his early forties, narrow-faced and slender, wearing a sport coat over a white shirt. His tie was undone, and he looked like someone who had just gotten off work and wanted nothing better than to kick back for the night, except that this little crisis was threatening to disrupt his peace and quiet.

"Hey, Dick," he called out calmly, getting Yanders's attention. "What's going on?"

Yanders held his ax protectively before him with one hand, using the other to point a warning finger at his neighbor. "You stay out of this, Vinnie."

"How can I do that?" Vincent replied, still keeping his voice as neutral as possible. "All these people here, all this racket? I've got work to do at home today, and I can't do it until things calm down, can I?"

"Yes," Leila Yanders said, picking up on Vincent's cues. She looked tearfully up at her husband, trying to play down his rage. "Richie, he's right. We don't have to make a circus out of this. We can talk this out, just the two of us. Okay?"

By way of response, Yanders abruptly stabbed the ax through a nearby window, shattering glass onto the ground. When Vincent Hobbs continued to step forward, Yanders hopped down the steps and forced him back with a vicious swipe. "Stay out of this! I'm tellin' ya!"

Vincent retreated to the edge of the crowd and watched helplessly as Yanders took another step and splintered the wooden mailbox near the front curb. He picked up a few of the pieces and threw them back at his wife, howling, "There's half the mailbox. How we doing so far?"

"Richie, please..."

"'Richie, please,'" Yanders mocked. "It's too late for that, Leila. Too damn late!"

Yanders took a modified batting stance and looked as if he was about to take a home run swing, using his wife's head as the ball. Suddenly a shot thundered through the night, and Yanders staggered slightly as a .45 ACP round slammed into the ax handle just above his fingers. Dumbfounded, he looked in the direction the shot had come from.

"You don't want me to have to fire this again," Gadgets Schwarz said as he stepped into view a few yards away from Vincent Hobbs. Casually dressed in stone-washed denims and a navy windbreaker, Schwarz was holding a Government Model Colt .45 in front of him. Schwarz knew the weapon as well as he knew his phone number, and when he shifted the gun so that he was aiming at Yanders's chest, he told Yanders, "This close I can put a hole in you big enough for that ax to fit through. Be smart and stay in one piece, okay?"

Yanders quickly recovered from his surprise and lunged to his wife's side, using her as a shield. He pressed the cold blade of the ax against her trembling cheek. "Beat it, mister," he warned Schwarz, "or *she's* the one who won't stay in one piece. Got that?"

Schwarz quickly assessed the situation and took a slow step backward, although he kept his gun trained on the couple. "Let's try and have a happy ending here, why don't we?"

"Shut up!" Yanders barked. "And get that gun out of my face! Who the hell are you, anyway?"

"He's my partner," Pol Blancanales called out as he emerged from behind the Yanderses' trailer. Like Schwarz, he was packing a .45 and had it pointed at the axman's face.

"And who are you?" Yanders roared with outrage, clutching his wife closer to him for protection. Tears rolled down the woman's cheeks and she sobbed with hopeless abandon.

"I'm your marriage counselor," Blancanales said as he inched along the side of the trailer. "How about we try to talk out this little problem you're having, hmmm?"

"No!" Yanders shouted. His eyes darted back and forth, taking in Schwarz, then Blancanales. "I'm through talking! Now get away, both of you!"

"What about me?"

Carl Lyons had managed to steal up behind Yanders and was less than a yard away when he spoke. Startled, Yanders lowered the ax slightly as he turned to glance over his shoulder. All he saw of Lyons was the blur of Ironman's hand heading straight for him. Before he could react, the well-placed karate blow took the fight out of Yanders, loosening his grip on consciousness and sending him in a headlong sprawl to the ground. The ax fell harmlessly to his side.

"He'll be okay in a few minutes," Lyons assured the woman as he began to untie the ropes that bound her to the post. "How about you? You going to be all right?"

Leila was still wild-eyed with fear, and it was all she could do to weakly bob her head. Rubbing her wrists where the bindings had chafed her flesh, she stared down at her husband. "I didn't really want a divorce," she whispered huskily. "I just wanted him to stop his drinking."

"Well, with any luck he'll remember some of this and it'll give him something to think about," Lyons told her.

By then some of the other neighbors were coming forward, and the three men of Able Team decided to turn matters over to them and to the police officers who were just pulling onto the scene, cruiser sirens blaring and rooftop lights throwing their spastic lights off the sides of the trailers. The teammates broke away from the crowd, seeking out Vincent Hobbs, who stood back near the driveway leading to his nearby trailer.

"I see you guys haven't lost your touch," Hobbs told them. "That was good work."

"Aw, shucks," Lyons drawled with false humility. "We just do what comes natural."

"Besides," Schwarz piped in, giving Hobbs a slight poke in the ribs, "what better way to start off your bachelor party than with a little taste of the wonders of married life, eh?"

Hobbs looked at the three men uncertainly. "I guess you guys didn't get my message at the airport. Sorry, but the party's off...."

VINCENT HOBBS and Able Team went back years, to the founding of Stony Man Farm, the rural Virginia compound in the heart of the Blue Ridge Mountains that served as the major nerve center for one of the nation's most clandestine special forces.

Able Team was the three-man unit invariably plugged into any domestic dirty-dealings that required priority, no-holds-barred tactics and the kind of neutralization that nailed wrongdoers without providing them with the chance to wriggle off the hook through the legal loopholes and constitutional vagaries that frustrated the efforts of so many other enforcement agencies forced to do business under a more scrutinizing eye. Surrounding the Team was a small army of backup personnel, ranging from head of operations Hal Brognola on down to various mechanics and security people charged with guarding the grounds.

Vincent Hobbs had been one of the Farm's unsung heroes, not only a crack chef who had supervised the preparation of the meals for whoever might be at the facility on any given day, but also a gardener of extraordinary talent. He had seen to it that the grounds were sufficiently maintained to support the belief that the Farm was a mere country estate belonging to some well-heeled entrepreneur. Remarkably, however, despite his talent in these two fields, Hobbs's true avocation was for writing, and three years ago he'd left Stony Man Farm when he'd received an offer to join the city desk at the *Las Vegas Herald*. He still kept in touch with those men he'd become close to back in Virginia, including Able Team, and whenever any of them passed through town, there were inevitable get-togethers for one of Hobbs's legendary homemade dinners and long talks about the "old times" back at Stony Man. Accordingly, it wasn't surprising that Able Team had pulled some time off to hit Vegas when Hobbs informed them that he'd decided to marry the paper's circulation manager.

The plan had called for a bachelor party that evening with the wedding on the weekend, but as the Team gathered in Hobbs's trailer across the way from the dispersing melodrama between the Yanderses, Vincent explained the reason there'd been a change of agenda.

"It's my nephew," Hobbs told them once he'd seen to it that his old friends were seated comfortably and had drinks in hand. The trailer was huge, sparsely but tastefully furnished with blond wood chairs and sofas covered in a material sporting high-tech motifs. A Duraflame log burned brightly in a cast-iron hearth, warding off the late-night chill.

"Last night he went out to a job interview over near the downtown tracks," Hobbs went on, "only there wasn't any interview. Turns out he stumbled onto the tail end of a warehouse robbery, and whoever called him about the interview also saw to it that the gun used in the robbery could be traced back to me. And now—"

"Whoa, hold on, Vinnie," Blancanales interjected. "Run that past us again. A gun of yours was used in the robbery?"

Hobbs nodded dejectedly. "It was stolen from my trailer here... I think the same day I went to pick up Billy at the train station when he rode down from Carson City. It must have been lifted by someone who knew I was taking him under my supervision."

"Any idea why?" Lyons asked.

"Why frame him? Easy," Hobbs said. "He's an easy target. Just out of jail, not much money to his name... you know the way it is. Poor kid made a mistake and he comes here with two strikes against him already. Then this..."

Lyons finished his drink and set the glass aside. "I take it they caught him and threw the book at him."

"No, not at all," Hobbs said. "See, when he showed up, he found the body of a guard who'd just been shot, then my gun. Before he had much of a chance to make any sense of it, the cops showed up and he ran. Almost got himself gunned down, but he managed to get away."

Blancanales looked around the trailer. "You aren't hiding him out here, are you?"

Hobbs shook his head. "No, he was staying here up until last night, but he hasn't been back since it happened."

"Then how did you know that he—"

"He called me late last night," Vincent said. He stared at his drink a moment, gently rattling the ice cubes against the sides of the glass. "He wouldn't say where he was calling from, but he sounded cold and scared. My guess is he's living off the streets somewhere."

"If he's innocent, he should just turn himself in and let things get sorted out," Lyons suggested.

"I tried to tell him that, but he wouldn't listen," Vincent agreed. "I can't really say as I blame him, either." Hobbs drained his drink and reached for the bottle resting on the bar. He caught himself at the last minute and refrained from refilling the glass. He licked his lips a moment, then looked at the three men before him.

"You see, when Billy was in prison, he was... you know what happens to young kids if they go in there with any semblance of vulnerability. Sexual abuse, random beatings. He paid one hell of a price for what he did. When I picked him up a couple of weeks ago after he got out, he vowed that he'd never let that happen to him again." Hobbs went to the window of the kitchen area and glanced out at an open field that stretched behind the trailer park. He swallowed hard. "I'm just afraid that if the police catch him, he'll do everything he can to see that they kill him rather than put him back behind bars."

Lyons looked at his two partners. Without so much as a word passing between them, it was clear that they were of one mind as to what needed to be done.

"Well, Vinnie," he told Hobbs, "I guess that we're just going to have to put our heads together and find a way to get to your nephew first."

2

There had once been a time when Ned Farrow had received preferential treatment at the casinos because he was mistaken for Ernest Borgnine, but in recent years he'd lost interest in pretense and had hidden most of his ruddy face behind a salt-and-pepper beard. His hair had thinned considerably as well, so he had also taken to wearing chalk-white Stetsons with hatbands of silver and turquoise. Topped off with an alpaca-lined suede overcoat, Farrow now looked less like a refugee from *McHale's Navy*, more like a grizzled landlubber raised on the range. He still got good service on the Strip, but now it was based on his own reputation as one of the feistiest and most successful bounty hunters in all of Nevada, if not the entire United States.

He did a lot of his business with casino owners anxious to catch up with folks who thought that by disappearing they might be able to duck some hefty tab left behind in the wake of a losing streak at the tables. Ned Farrow got results, especially when his clients weren't too particular as to the methods he used in plying his trade. Some of his exploits had become the stuff of local legends, and he took care never to confirm or deny the more outrageous tales, even when they might take great liberties with the truth. In particular, he relished keeping a straight face whenever talk turned to men he'd gunned down during shoot-outs in the Nevada wilds. Been known to happen, he'd say about such incidents. Around town there was an unofficial motto that served as his calling card to prospective clients: You want 'em alive, you want 'em dead, either way's all right with Ned.

Farrow lived five miles off the Strip in one of the newest housing developments that were continually reaching outward from the city's core like probing appendages of some gargantuan amoeba. Mesquite Haven would eventually be a 203-unit complex butting up against a proposed golf course and shopping plaza. Now it was something of a last frontier, consisting of a handful of completed homes and partitioned plots of land awaiting the influx of fresh capital so that they, too, could be transformed into residences for some well-heeled croupier or Vegas show girl looking for a nice big home within driving distance of work.

Farrow had deliberately chosen a plot at the back corner of the lot, with his property inching close to a rugged arroyo that was dry all but those few days a year when torrential downpours would fill the desert with seething streams of floodwater. This morning, as he walked out the back door in his customary outfit, he stopped to gaze at his eastward view, which was unobstructed by any trace of civilization. There was only the vast expanse of parched desert, barren save for tufts of hearty mesquite and, far off against the horizon, the soft rolling hills behind which lay Lake Mead and Hoover Dam. The sun had just cleared the hilltops, turning the flat terrain a warm shade of gold.

Nice day to kick some ass, the bounty hunter reflected as he turned up the collar of his coat. A faint, chilly breeze was rolling in from the desert, and a huge antenna creaked slightly as it wavered in place atop the roof of Farrow's house.

Crossing his freshly sodded lawn, Farrow squinted against the sun's glare and unlocked the back gate. Old rail ties blocked out a set of steps leading down a steep-pitched grade to the wash.

In his right hand, Farrow was carrying a .454 Casull, won the previous night during a four-hour poker marathon in a private room at the Sands Hotel. He'd wanted such a weapon since he'd first heard of its production three years ago, and he couldn't wait to try it out.

At the base of the arroyo, Farrow spied tracks in the soft, sandy ground. The larger marks had been left by a kit fox, one of hundreds that roamed the area. The smaller tracks were not only the imprint of feet but also of a body and tail dragged along the surface. Gila monster, Farrow thought to himself as he followed the tracks, seeking out the creature's burrow. He had yet to spot one of the lizards, which were nocturnal and therefore usually tucked away in their lairs by dawn, but he'd seen other evidence of their presence near his home, usually in the form of egg fragments or the half-eaten remains of small rodents that had somehow failed to elude the Gila's nightly forays.

Once he found the small, fist-sized opening in the embankment, Farrow backtracked to a spot several yards away, where he'd placed a wire cage in front of another, similar hole. He transferred the cage to the new location, then followed the wash away from his home until he rounded a knoll that would serve as a sound buffer.

Because this strip of land was often frequented by vagrants or mischievous teenagers, there was always a ready supply of trash that could be used for target practice. Farrow gathered up a handful of beer cans and pop bottles, setting them up in a neat row atop the rusting hulk of a Sears oven someone had dumped in the desert years ago. He paced off thirty-five steps, then paused to slip on a pair of shooting gloves. Padded slightly in the manner of those used for handball, the gloves were intended to help blunt the trauma a gun like the Casull could wreak on one's palm and fingers with the force of its recoil. Farrow's fingers poked through openings in the glove, allowing him to get a reasonably good grip of the weapon. At slightly more than three pounds, it had a heft that spoke of power. But if there were any doubts in his mind as to the potency of the Casull, they were dismissed as he pulled a fifty-dollar box of twenty .454 shells from his coat. The bullets were so large that the Casull's bloated cylinder could hold only five of them at a time.

"Okay, baby, let's talk," Farrow mumbled as he stuffed wads of cotton into his ears and then assumed a firing stance. Peering down the gun's sights, he focused on the distant oven and its row of targets. He'd used the oven for target practice before and had even taken the trouble to screw on a plate of quarter-inch steel over the utility drawer. The plate bore numerous dents from the impact of stray .44 and .357 blasts. On a whim, Farrow lowered the gun and took aim at the plate, then squeezed the trigger.

With an authoritative whomp, the first bullet charged out of the barrel at a muzzle velocity of two thousand feet per second, nearly double the force of the .44 Magnum Dirty Harry had once boasted to be the world's most powerful handgun. And, whereas Farrow's own .44 had only dented the steel plate on the oven drawer, the Casull's slug bored through, not only leaving a tidy hole in the plate but also wrenching the entire oven with so much force that the cans and bottles atop it wobbled sharply, half of them falling over and back into the sand.

Raising the gun slightly, Farrow fired a second shot, obliterating one of the cans. His entire right hand ached from just the two shots, and the kick had sent shock waves riding all the way up his arm and into his shoulders.

"Goddamn," he muttered in awe, staring down at the gun. "Man, you are one deadly piece."

As he climbed back up the wooden steps and reentered his yard, Farrow saw a telltale cloud of dust on the unpaved road leading to his house. Circling to the driveway, he made out the gleaming contours of a dark gray Mercedes limousine.

"Burlington," he muttered to himself. He unbuttoned his coat long enough to slip the mighty Casull inside the waistline of his designer jeans, then took a few steps down the driveway to meet the arriving vehicle. The Mercedes had tinted windows, making it impossible to gauge how many people were inside. Once the limo was in the driveway, a back window hissed down to reveal Wesley Burlington, a misleadingly frail-looking man with wire-rimmed bifocals perched on a thin, hooked nose. He wore a three-piece suit that matched the Mercedes's gray tones and his bony fingers were clasped around the ivory handle of a walking cane.

"Good morning, Ned," Burlington wheezed over the idling purr of the engine.

"'Lo, Mr. B.," Farrow responded casually, bending slightly so he could look inside the limo and see that Burlington was traveling alone except for the chauffeur, a broad-shouldered Jamaican with short dreadlocks spilling out from under his narrow-brimmed cap. The driver's attention was focused straight ahead and he made no effort to acknowledge Farrow's presence.

"We have a small problem, Ned."

"The robbery didn't come off?" Farrow asked.

"Oh, it did," Burlington said. "The problem's with the Hobbs boy. I'm afraid he managed to get away before the police could get their hands on him."

"Shit."

"Yes, it is rather unfortunate. But I don't think he'll have gotten far." Burlington reached into his coat and withdrew an envelope, passing it to Farrow. "I'm sure you can take care of him, Ned."

Ned pried open the envelope and glanced at the neat stack of fifty-dollar bills. He smiled thinly and told the older man, "I'll take care of him."

3

Prior to arriving in Nevada, Able Team had made arrangements to spend their Vegas stay at the Dromedary, a low-key casino/hotel complex located between the downtown core and the Strip. They had three adjacent rooms in the rear bungalows, which were plain blocky structures stretching back to an alley that was also used by various retail outlets.

Blancanales woke up a little before nine to the sound of construction crews remodeling a dry-cleaning store just down the block. After turning on the television to mask the noise, Pol trudged into the bathroom long enough to splash water on his face and lather up for a quick shave. That finished, he began dressing as he put a call through to his associates. No one answered in either Lyons's or Schwarz's room.

They're probably at the slots already, he thought as he hung up the phone and finished putting on his pants and flannel shirt. For someone who was willing to put his life on the line at a moment's notice, Blancanales surprisingly lacked any gambling urges when it came to games of chance, and he hadn't shared his teammates' enthusiasm about doing a little time in the casinos while they were in town for Vinnie's wedding.

Maybe it had something to do with his upbringing. A childhood spent eking out a meager existence in the barrios of San Ysidro and East Los Angeles had ingrained in his mind the idea that there was no such thing as "fun money" and nothing commendable about the pursuit of frivolity or gambling to make a quick buck. His parents had been adamant about instilling such a perspective in the minds of their children. Even now Jorges and Anna Blancanales refused to allow lottery tickets to be sold at the small market they'd recently bought into in the Los Angeles suburb of Canoga Park. Money earned without sweat is the currency of ruin, Pol's father liked to say.

The phone rang as Blancanales was squeezing his feet into a pair of ostrich-skin cowboy boots. He grabbed the receiver on the third ring.

"You guys had your fill yet?" he asked.

"What's that, Pol?" came the distant voice on the line, obviously coming from somewhere farther away than the rooms next door.

"Oh, nothing," Blancanales said, recognizing the voice of Hal Brognola, the avuncular chief of operations back at Stony Man Farm. "How's the weather back there, Hal?"

"Cold as sin, but at least the ground's solid beneath my feet." Brognola chuckled, referring to one of the Team's most recent exploits, which had sent the men and most of their backup personnel to deal with a band of renegade Red Chinese terrorists who had been using stolen nuclear charges to trigger earthquakes along fragile California fault lines. It had been one of Stony Man's roughest assignments, with the lives of literally thousands, if not millions, at stake. Fortunately, the perpetrators had been apprehended before the casualty list had even begun to realize its dark potential. In consideration of the long hours the men had put into that mission and one in San Diego that had followed close on its heels, Brognola had willingly granted them the time off for their sojourn to Vegas...subject to any last-minute change of plans warranted by the unnerving fact that the world's scum seldom extended the courtesy of calling a truce on their machinations so that men like those in Able Team could fully unwind after any given run-in. Today was to be no exception, and Blancanales suspected as much from the tone in the head Fed's voice.

"So, Chief, let me guess," Pol said. "You're calling with another one of your 'As-long-as-you-guys-are-in-town-maybe-you-can-tend-to-a-little-business-for-me' propositions, right?"

There was a pause on the line, then Brognola replied, "Have I really become that predictable?"

"Afraid so. Let's have it."

"Well, I *did* get your message from Bear about wanting to help out Vincent, and of course you know that the Farm will back you all the way in doing anything we can to help him out. But, yes, there *is* another matter, too..."

Blancanales pulled out a complimentary pen and some Dromedary stationery featuring the casino's logo of a camel wearing sunglasses. He scribbled notes as Brognola outlined a situation that had recently come to his attention.

"We've made good contacts in Vegas over the years," Brognola explained, "and for the most part, word is the authorities are making a lot of headway keeping the casinos clean, especially in terms of organized crime involvement.''

"Yeah, I know all about that," Blancanales said. "RICO laws, SEC rulings, having the places go public and answer to shareholders...the whole nine yards, right?"

"That pretty well sums it up, for the most part," Brognola said. "But let's face it, with all that money floating around Vegas, it's just too much of a temptation for the Mob to resist, and there's always some kind of action going down with families trying to weasel into the picture with some scam that'll let them get their hands on some easy skim."

"I hope you're not going to tell me we're holing up in a Mafia hothouse." Blancanales chuckled.

"No, nothing like that, Pol. It's just that the Justice Department's organized-crime task force working out of Vegas has been pulling a lot of overtime lately, and the feeling we get is that maybe something bigger than usual is shaping up somewhere down the pike. Possibly even the biggest Mob action out that way since the sixties."

"And you want us to throw in our two cents' worth over a couple of days and put the whole syndicate out of commission, eh, Hal?"

"Please, Pol, it's bad enough I have to stomach sarcasm from Carl. Don't give me the business, okay?"

"Okay. So what do you want from us?"

"Well, the thing that ties in most directly to Able Team is the fact that it looks as if our old friends in ARC have reared their heads yet again, this time in North Las Vegas."

"ARC? Are you kidding?" Blancanales couldn't believe what he was hearing. "How many times do we have to lop their heads off, anyway?"

To date, Able Team had twice gone head-to-head with the Aryan Right Coalition, a white supremacist group with a paramilitary bent toward violence that made the Ku Klux Klan seem like the Boy Scouts in comparison. The first battle had climaxed in a brutal shoot-out during which the Team had prevented ARC founder Delbert Gunther and his inner circle from poisoning a New York City water station with nuclear waste, and the second, equally explosive confrontation had taken place down in bayou country in and around New Orleans. It had been thought that the latter effort had effectively eliminated what was left of the ARC's membership, putting behind bars those few hate-mongering souls who hadn't been put underground after the dust had settled.

"From what information we've been able to get on this latest incarnation," Brognola divulged, "it seems that we're really dealing with people who've just adopted the ARC name and agenda, and not with original members."

"Passing the arson torch."

"In a manner of speaking, yes."

"Why in Vegas?" Blancanales asked.

"According to the task force, it looks like the Mob helped this batch of misfits get off the ground and currently has them on a leash of sorts."

"Their own private goon squad."

"Exactly," Brognola said. "A couple of weeks ago, there was a bombing of a black-owned liquor distributorship off Bonanza Road. Three killed, eight injured. Word is some Mob clan must be getting ready to make some kind of major power play and wanted to send out a message that they'll be playing hardball with anyone who tries to work their turf. It fits their standard pattern, at any rate."

"Certainly sounds like a familiar scenario," Pol agreed. "And what kind of scum are in this new ARC?"

"That's the really sad part," Brognola said. "From what few descriptions the task force has uncovered, it looks like the work of teenagers. Skinheads, you know?"

"Yeah, I know," Blancanales said. "My folks tell me the same thing's cropping up out in L.A. Lot of bored white punks from the suburbs with too little direction and no drive."

"So, anyway," Brognola concluded, "I'll give you the name of the people to contact there. The skids have been greased so they'll be more than happy to give you as much slack as you need to go about your business. If you could check out both the Bureau connections and their police counterparts, you should be able to have the big picture brought into full focus. Trust me, they'll be grateful for any help you can give them."

"Fair enough," Blancanales said. He jotted down the names and phone numbers. "Odds are these people will be able to help us out trying to get to Vinnie's nephew, too, so it should work out nicely."

"Good, good to hear it," Brognola said. "Of course, you realize that I also have your best interests in mind. I figure the busier I keep you guys while you're in Vegas, the less money you're going to blow in the casinos."

"You don't have to worry about me on that count, Chief."

"I know that, but I can't say the same for your buddies."

Just then there was a knock on the door. Blancanales carried the phone over and opened the door. Lyons and Schwarz walked in looking tired and irritated.

"I think they've already had their first taste of the agony of defeat," Blancanales told Brognola.

4

Billy Hobbs hadn't slept the past two nights and it showed. His eyes were red, his face unshaven, and a bone-weary fatigue made his movements slow and erratic. Periodically his overwrought nerves would short-circuit on him, sending a sharp jolt along his spine and making him twitch with involuntary spasms. Deep in his stomach he felt a raw, knotting sensation that was due as much to fear as hunger. When he dared to steal from the shadows of a small decrepit tool shack near the tracks and spend a few moments crouched in the morning sunlight, he tried to sort out the blur of the past thirty-six hours.

After eluding the police at the site of the Global Imports robbery, Billy had crept along side streets until he had reached the edge of town, where he found refuge amid the twisted remains of old car wrecks in a sprawling salvage yard. He'd stayed there until the yard had opened in the morning, then he'd spent most of the day wandering the back streets of North Las Vegas. He was sure that if anyone saw him he would be easily mistaken for just another transient. He'd spent what little money he had buying food at a convenience store, and he'd bartered that food for a chance to spend the second night in the company of half a dozen other homeless men who'd taken over a deserted gas station on West Nathan and turned it into their makeshift shelter. His call to his uncle had been from a phone near the station, and shortly after hanging up on Vinnie Hobbs's pleas that he turn himself in, Billy had been forced to flee his would-be lodgings when a police cruiser had pulled up to the station and a pair of officers had gotten out to roust the squatters. Back on his own, he'd worked his way back to the salvage yard, where he lay down for a few hours but was unable to sleep. There was just too much on his mind.

· And now, several hours later, he felt as if his head was about to split from all the frantic thoughts bounding about inside his skull. There seemed to be no way out of his dilemma. As he'd told his uncle, turning himself in was out of the question. He'd rather die than face the many shameful abuses he'd been forced to endure during his years behind bars in Carson City. The slightest recollection of those degradations was enough to raise bile in his throat and turn his stomach to the point where he felt he would vomit if he had anything left inside him.

"Damn them," he whimpered, feeling a lone tear roll down his cheek, collecting grime from his days on the run. "Damn them."

He stood and retreated to the shadows as a train thundered by him on the tracks. He watched the cars rush by, wondering if he should try to board one of them. The thought intrigued him, and the more he dwelt on it, the more attractive it became. Be like a hobo, hitch a free ride out of town and not get off until somewhere far down the line. Yeah, maybe there was something to that. Get out of the state, put Vegas behind him, wait things out. In time maybe they'd find the real gunman who'd killed that guard; then he would be in the clear and could come back. Or maybe he would just stay away regardless, come up with a new identity, try to make a new life for himself.

Worth a try, he finally convinced himself, drawing in a deep breath as he moved away from the shack and tried to focus his full attention on the passing railcars. The train was in the process of leaving town, so it hadn't picked up its full speed. Taking long strides parallel to the tracks, he concentrated on the rhythm of the cars' movement, then broke into a jog and inched closer. Once he had built up his own momentum to the point where he was almost matching the speed of the cars, he eyed the ladder rungs of the nearest boxcar and extended his arms, reaching, reaching out until his fingers were mere inches away.

"Now!" he shouted, putting every last remnant of strength into leaping forward and upward, closing his fingers tightly around one of the middle rungs. He immediately felt an incredible jerking sensation as he was pulled along by the rolling train, and for a fleeting second he feared his arms were going to be wrenched from their sockets. When they weren't, he struggled to pull himself up and shift his dangling feet to the lowest rungs of the ladder. He had underestimated the sheer strength and agility required for such a feat, however, and as the train continued to pick up speed, Billy felt himself losing his grip. He was certain that any second his legs were going to swing under the train and be crushed by the massive steel wheels.

As the train rounded a slight bend in the tracks, centrifugal force eased his legs away from the wheels and Billy let go of the rungs, pushing himself away from the boxcar in the same motion. He opened his mouth to scream but struck the ground first. The wind was knocked from his lungs as he tumbled over and over, cinders biting into his flesh, until finally he came to a stop at the bottom of the sloping grade the tracks rested on. Once the last car had passed by, taking the train's shadow with it, the sun's rays fell warmly over Billy as he lay still, bleeding and bruised.

AS HE FELT HIMSELF struggling to return to consciousness sometime later, Billy's mind snagged on a memory, no doubt one of the last thoughts he'd been having before falling from the train.

It was the day of his release from prison in Carson City. He was just down the block, a free man in a small greasy spoon located near the train depot. For his first meal after three years behind bars, he'd splurged on a double cheeseburger, onion rings, coleslaw, potato salad and the biggest chocolate milk shake he'd ever seen. Sitting in a corner booth, he'd devoured the meal with greedy abandon while dividing his attention between reading the *Carson City News* and watching the people who filtered in and out of the diner. At one point a short, wiry man in a cheap double-breasted suit had sauntered in and sat at the counter, ordering coffee and a slice of pie. Billy recognized him. His name was Ralph Calno and he'd paid several visits to the prison in recent weeks, always to see the same man, Vegas Bobby Sumur, a syndicate heavy doing time while appealing a sentence of thirty-six years for bribery, extortion and attempted murder, all crimes perpetrated downstate. Since much of the abuse Billy had suffered had been at the hands of prisoners with known links to both Sumur and Calno, he had no desire to mix with the mafioso on the outside. Quickly finishing his meal, Billy had retreated to the diner rest room and concealed himself in one of the stalls.

While he was waiting there, Billy had heard the flunky just outside the bathroom, making a phone call. Calno was trying to be as vague and cryptic in his conversation as possible, but from what little Billy could make out, he couldn't help but understand the bottom line—contracts were being put out on witnesses who would be testifying against Vegas Bobby Sumur once his appeal came through and there was a second trial.

Billy waited another ten minutes before leaving the bathroom, but to his horror he found that Calno was still at the counter, nursing a cup of coffee. As discreetly as possible, Billy had paid his bill and slipped out the front door, hoping to get back to the train station unmolested. However, Calno left the diner moments later and quickly caught up with him.

"Long time in the crapper, sonny," the short man had told Billy as he fell into step beside him.

"Diarrhea," Billy lied.

"Better to run at the ass than the mouth," Calno said. "Know what I mean?"

"I don't want any trouble," Billy had told the man, lengthening his stride as he neared the depot. Calno stayed with him.

"That's good to know, Billy."

Hobbs had been stunned to hear the man use his name. He stopped in front of the depot and looked at Calno, trying hard not to show any fear in his eyes. It didn't work. "How...how did you know my—"

"I'm in the information business," Calno had told him. "I know your name, I know where you're going, and I know who your parole officer's going to be. Just think of me as your Big Brother, okay?"

"Uh, yeah," Billy had managed to stammer. "Sure."

"I know your uncle, too," Calno said. "Nice guy. Wants to look after you, I hear."

"How do you know all this?"

Calno pretended he hadn't heard Billy and went on, "Be nice for you to get a chance to look after him, don't you think? See to it he stays healthy."

A train security officer had stepped out of the main entrance to the depot and paused to light a cigarette near the other two men. Calno grinned and patted Billy on the shoulder. "Good luck, kid. Keep that nose clean and mind your own business and I got a feeling you and your uncle will make out okay."

With that, Calno had walked off, leaving Billy to enter the depot alone. He hadn't said anything to the security guard, and he hadn't said anything to his uncle when he reached Vegas later that day, even when Vincent's handgun had turned up missing. As far as the world was concerned, Billy Hobbs didn't know anything about any phone conversation about killing witnesses, and he planned to keep it that way.

Or did he?

As Billy shook off the memory of his encounter with Ralph Calno, and as full consciousness tried to return, he realized at once that somehow the mobster was behind the theft of his uncle's gun and the call that had lured him to the Global Imports warehouse. He also knew that the plan had probably been for him to be gunned down at the scene, not only so he would take the rap for the robbery, but also so he would be forever silenced before he'd had a chance to divulge what he'd heard of that phone conversation at the diner back in Carson City.

"B . . . b . . . bastard!" he cursed Ralph Calno as he opened his eyes.

"Hey, I was just trying to help!"

The second voice belonged to a woman in her early forties with peroxide blond hair, tanned and wearing a bulky sweater that seemed out of place with her short leather skirt. There were broken gaps in her fishnet stockings and scuffs on the large simulated leather purse dangling from her shoulder. She stood over Billy near a cluster of large packing crates stacked near the rail tracks.

"I dragged you outta the sun so you wouldn't get a stroke or something," the woman continued, "so don't be callin' me names."

When Billy tried to move, he became aware of a sharp, throbbing pain that enveloped his entire body. He could feel that his face was bruised and swollen, as was most of his left side. But he was alive, which was more than he had counted on during that split second between the time he'd lost his grip on the train and the time he'd hit the ground.

"Sorry," he managed to sputter as he sat up, grimacing from the agony of that small movement. "I . . . I wasn't talking to you."

"Well, good deal. Look, I gotta go. Late for work as it is."

The woman started off. Billy called out to her, "Wait! I'm hurting. I need—"

"Hey, I ain't the Salvation Army," she called over her shoulder. "You need to go lick your wounds, try that old packing plant behind you. Regular Bum Hilton, and no slots to lose your money on." She laughed sinisterly and crossed the tracks before disappearing from view behind the elevated hump of the rail bed.

Billy stayed put for a few minutes, trying to decide how long he'd been unconscious. The sun was directly overhead, so he calculated that it was at least noon. Not that time mattered much to him at this point. He was just thankful to be free and alive despite his blunder with the train. Touching himself, he took heart that maybe he hadn't broken any bones. Maybe if he just holed up in the packing plant for a while he could wait out the worst of his pain and plot a new course of action.

With consummate effort, he got to his feet and began limping toward the large structure, fifty yards away. After two steps he froze, reaching behind him and patting the back pocket of his pants. His wallet. It was gone. Eyes wide with shock, Billy looked around him. No trace of it.

He glanced across the tracks, just in time to see the woman in the sweater squirming through a gap in a cyclone fence separating the rails from the downtown casinos. "You bitch!" he called out, spitting blood from a cracked lip. His voice was weak, no match for another train that thundered down the tracks, coming from the opposite direction as the one he'd tried to jump earlier.

This time he let the train go by.

5

"Trust me," Carl Lyons said. "I've been in your shoes, and I know that these special task forces are always undermanned and overworked."

"Oh?" Police Sergeant James Alper raised an eyebrow as he leaned back in his chair and crossed his arms. A plump cigar was wedged between his large nicotine-stained teeth, which were roughly the same color as his light, close-cropped hair. He had the sort of ageless face that allowed him to pass as being anywhere between thirty-five and fifty—whichever age circumstances called for. His gray eyes were filled with skepticism as he gave Lyons a thorough once-over.

"And exactly what sort of experience do you have in this sort of work?"

Lyons leaned forward in his seat, propping his elbows on the front of Alper's desk. Between the desk and the two men, there wasn't much room left in the cramped office, whose long window afforded a partial view of the distant Strip. "I did a stint with the Los Angeles Police Department back in the seventies," Lyons explained, "and from there I was plugged into an outfit like yours. Same setup. You get a few extra bucks, a separate office and orders to go after the cream of the crap, no holds barred except that you're supposed to work in conjunction with the Feds. A losing proposition for the most part, because you still don't have half the resources the bad guys do. You work your ass off night and day for months on end and what little dent you make in the underworld isn't enough to get the men upstairs off your back, 'cause they're expecting miracles.''

Alper took the cigar from his mouth and blew a cloud of smoke across the desk as he uncrossed his arms and grinned at Lyons. ''Yeah, sounds like you know the score, all right. I already got orders from the Bureau boys to play ball with you, but I figured if we saw things eye to eye it'd be easier on both of us.''

''Fair enough.''

''You talked to the Bureau guys here?'' Alper inquired.

Lyons shook his head. ''Timing's not so good on that front. They're split up right now, half of them up around Tahoe and Carson City and the others back in Washington for some conference.''

''Oh, yeah, that's right,'' Alper recalled. ''So then basically it comes down to our end here at the station.''

''Yep,'' Lyons said. ''Should hopefully make things a little less complicated at any rate. Less red tape and all that.''

''True.'' Alper swiveled his chair around and began rummaging through a file cabinet as Lyons glanced at merit plaques on the walls bearing the sergeant's name. From the looks of it, Alper had more than earned his stripes over the years.

''There are three of you, right?'' Alper asked Lyons as he tried a different drawer of the cabinet. He found the file he was looking for and opened it on the desk. "Okay, let me see if we got this straight. If we get any leads on this Billy Hobbs, we're supposed to let you guys have first crack at bringing him in."

"That's it in a nutshell."

"And in return, you guys will throw in on our task force dealing with these Aryan Right quacks."

"Right again," Lyons said, glancing at the opened file in front of the sergeant. "So what do you have for us to go on?"

"Not much, I'm afraid," Alper confessed. He handed over a couple of sheets of paper. "Here's a map pinpointing incidents of vandalism attributable to the Aryan Right Coalition. The large circle indicates where the liquor distributorship was bombed. As you can see, there's no real set pattern or locale they're focusing on, other than the fact that they're most active in North Vegas."

The second sheet was a flier containing a lengthy racist diatribe and the ARC logo. As Lyons skimmed through it, Alper continued. "This was found stapled to a telephone pole next to where the bombing took place. Other copies have been mailed to the media, all from different post offices."

"Sick stuff," Lyons said, glancing up from the tract. "I'm for the First Amendment and all, but when I come across shit like this I want to shut somebody up, but good."

"Hopefully you'll get a chance to do that," Alper said, glancing at his watch. "Look, is there anything else I can help you with? I have another appointment coming up."

"Do you have extra copies of these?" Lyons asked, indicating the fliers.

"Yup. Go ahead and take those."

"Great." Lyons stood up. "One other thing ... any chance I can get my hands on the police report for that gun theft at Vincent Hobbs's trailer home?"

Alper tapped ash into a souvenir ashtray from one of the downtown casinos. He smiled sardonically at Lyons. "I can track it down for you, but you don't really think there's much worth looking into on that front, do you?"

"What do you mean?"

"I mean, it seems pretty obvious Billy Hobbs helped himself to that popgun as soon as he got to town and had it stashed away for that warehouse robbery."

"A little too obvious, if you ask me," Lyons said. "I think it was made to look that way. Think about it. If Billy really wanted to take a gun on the sly, he wouldn't have gone for his uncle's."

"Oh?"

"We happen to think Billy's innocent," Lyons said. "That's one of the main reasons we want to make sure he gets brought in in one piece. Somebody was out to frame him, and we aim to find out why."

Alper said, "Well, I wish you luck. I'll track down that report for you as soon as I can. Where are you staying?"

"The Dromedary."

Alper snorted. "The Dromedary? Must be on a tight budget, huh?"

"It serves our needs. We didn't come here to be pampered, anyway."

"Well, just a friendly word of advice," the cop told Lyons. "Their slot payoffs are the worst in the city. Avoid 'em like the plague."

Lyons was forced to grin. "Too bad we didn't have this conversation last night."

WITHIN TEN MINUTES of walking Lyons out of the police station, Sergeant Alper was halfway across town, slipping in the back entrance of the Caravan Hotel. Although it was still relatively early, the lobby was abuzz with slot players feeding coins into rows of one-armed bandits. Bells and beepers announced jackpots, however large or small, and the clatter of coins spilling down winner's chutes served as a further enticement to those debating whether or not to crack open another roll of nickels or quarters in hopes of reversing their fortunes. Off in the main casino, there was limited action at the baccarat and blackjack tables, and it looked as if some players were just about to get started at craps in front of the huge dollar spin wheel.

Alper had no interest in frittering away his time or money on these ventures, however. He knew from experience that the best way to handle Vegas as a gambler was to bypass the ground floor casino action and make the necessary arrangements to gain access to private suites elsewhere in the upper reaches of any given hotel. That was where the high rollers could indulge themselves without having to rub elbows with nickel-dime suburbanites from the Midwest who fancied a twenty-dollar stake as a hefty wager when spread out over a night of slot and board play.

Seeking out one of the floor managers lingering near the main change booth, Alper gave a brief, perfunctory nod and was led back through a private hallway to the service elevators.

"And how are you this morning, Sergeant?" the lean man in the burgundy suit asked.

"How many times do I have to tell you not to call me sergeant around here?" Alper snapped.

"Sorry, Mr. Alper. My mistake." The other man reached out with his key ring and activated the elevator closest to them. The doors hissed open and Alper stepped in. The floor manager remained in the hall, telling him, "They're in the usual place. Good luck to you."

"Yeah, right."

Alper reached inside his coat for a cellophane-wrapped cigar as the elevator door closed. He unwrapped the cigar slowly, trying to rein in his temper. He knew from experience that a lack of self-control led quickly to ruin in places like this. It was essential to always remain in command, in control.

Getting off at the third floor, Alper lit his cigar and puffed on it nonchalantly as he strolled down the corridor. Although part of the hotel, this section of hallway was off-limits to regular guests and housed most of the offices for the Caravan staff. When he reached the conference room, the sergeant pulled a money clip from his pocket and peeled off a five spot for the thick-chested man seated outside the door in a navy-and-gray security uniform. A .357 Magnum rested snugly in his waist holster.

"Open sesame, Earl," he said with a conspiratorial wink.

"You got it, Mr. Alper." Without getting up from his chair, the guard reached to his left and pulled the door open.

Smoke hung heavily in the conference room, rising from ashtrays at the elbows of the four men and a woman seated around a square table set near a plate-glass window. The view overlooked the Caravan's novelty courtyard petting zoo, where several camels and llamas grazed in the morning sun. Next to the window was a serving table laden with an assortment of breakfast rolls, fresh fruit, sandwiches and two urns filled with coffee. Alper started filling a small plate with rolls before Wes Burlington glanced over at him. "What's the good word, Jimmy?"

"Not so good this morning, Wes," Alper said.

"You met with those three men?" Ralph Calno asked as the sergeant pulled up to the table and tossed ten dollars into the kitty before sitting down. Calno had on a cheap suit similar to the one he'd worn up in Carson City a few days previously when he'd had his run-in with Billy Hobbs near the train station.

"Not all three of them," Alper said, nodding a greeting to the others at the table. Clint Dirry, a stocky, bearded man in his early fifties, was public relations head for the hotel/casino. Beside him sat thirty-one-year-old whiz kid Rick Fries, who had taken over running the hotel shortly after the imprisonment of Vegas Bobby Sumur. Sumur had called the casino's shots from the sidelines while trying to piece together his share of the action in town. The woman, Janice Kennesey, was in her mid-thirties, meticulously dressed in a beige business suit and holding a pearl-inlaid cigarette holder that matched her earrings and necklace.

She owned Global Imports, the firm whose warehouse had been victimized by the robbery a couple of nights before.

As Dirry started dealing a new round of five card stud, Alper went on, "I met this guy Lyons. Ex-LAPD. Seems to know how these task forces are supposed to work. All three belong to a special forces group called Able Team."

"How much trouble they figure to make?" Calno asked.

"Depends," Alper said. "From the sounds of it, they plan to stick around awhile. Worse yet, they know Vincent Hobbs and they've got this idea in their heads they're gonna prove that the kid's not behind the robbery."

"Just what we don't need is some outsiders sniffing around our business," Janice Kennesey grumbled as she bid on her king of hearts.

"Yeah, well I'll try to throw 'em off my scent as much as I can," Alper said, "but we all know these folks aren't morons. Remember what they did to the families back East last year?"

"We remember all too well," Dirry said.

The previous winter, Able Team had played a key roll in thwarting the Mob's attempt to spring a handful of its imprisoned dons by stealing a cache of volatile nerve gas and threatening to unleash it on Los Angeles if their demands weren't met. Concurrent with that effort, the Team had also helped shut down one of the West Coast Mob's primary outlets for the making and distribution of pornographic movies. Since that time, an unofficial price had been put on Able Team's collective head, although little effort had been made by the Mob to neutralize the Team.

Fries matched Kennesey's bid and raised her ten dollars as he told the group, "Maybe we should take the offensive. Get these fuckers back. Think of the clout it'd give us.

"We tell the families back East that we took them out, shit, it'd grease our skids on all those plans we got for expanding out of here. I say we go for it."

"I don't know," Kennesey said, matching the raised bid. She stubbed out her cigarette and replaced a fresh one in the holder. "I think we have to play it careful...same reason we aren't leaning on Vincent Hobbs. Anything happens to them and people are going to know we're behind it."

"Maybe yes, maybe no," Calno ventured. He glanced over at Alper. "You said these guys are looking to crack down on ARC, right?"

"Yeah," Alper said.

"Well, as long as we can keep the skinheads separate from us, anything they do doesn't have to reflect on us," Calno thought aloud. "Supposing these men get their asses ambushed by ARC and end up pushing daisies? We set things up so we have some of our people on the sidelines to make sure the skins get killed at the same time, the story ends there."

Burlington watched the cards being dealt around, showing no emotion when he ended up showing a pair of queens. He reached for the mound of bills in front of him and tossed a hundred-dollar bill into the pot. "It's worth considering, Ralph," he told Calno, "but let's take things one at a time. Before we do anything else, I want this Hobbs kid taken out of the picture so his tongue won't get a chance to go loose on him.''

"Farrow should be able to handle that soon enough,'' Fries said, matching Burlington's bid. The other players dropped out.

"Let's hope so,'' Burlington said. "With that kid out of the way, it will be a whole different ball game.''

6

Ned Farrow cruised the side streets of Vegas in his vintage '65 white Mustang convertible, top down, radio blaring the latest rock hit by Love and Rockets. He bobbed his head in time with the beat and doffed his Stetson whenever he happened to draw the attention of a woman walking the streets without an escort. In some other city such an incongruous image might have drawn wary stares or shouts of disapproval, but Vegas had a high tolerance for the outrageous, and the women he greeted more often than not waved back. Of course, on several occasions those women weren't strangers to Farrow, but rather local casino employees on their way to or from work.

Farrow had a reputation for paying well for information pertinent to any case he might be working on, and he was therefore able to use his Mustang as something of a roving office. He would call people over for a look at a photo of Billy Hobbs and ask if the young man had been seen in the area. In the event that he came up with a lead, there was the cellular phone next to his seat, which he could use to contact any one of the eleven free-lancers he kept on retainer for those assignments necessitating more legwork than he could handle alone.

By noon, Farrow had zigzagged the entire length of the Strip and followed the boulevard up into North Las Vegas, touching base with eight different street contacts, putting out the word on Billy Hobbs. No one had spotted the young man as yet, but Farrow wasn't all that surprised. He expected better results once his freelancers had a chance to canvass the outskirts, particularly west of the railroad yards.

For lunch, Farrow stopped off at an outdoor hot dog stand located just up the block from the downtown police station. Sergeant Alper had called him earlier in the morning to arrange a rendezvous, and Farrow found the officer seated on a bench near the back wall, already halfway through a chili cheese dog.

"What say, lawman?" Farrow drawled as he sat down across from Alper with his order of two soft beef tacos. "You clean Burlington out after I left?"

"Don't I wish," Alper groaned. "I was up two grand till the last few hands, then he cleaned my clocks, but good. He must mark the deck somehow."

"Yeah, sure."

"At least he left me with enough spare change for lunch."

"Easy come, easy go."

"Ain't that the truth."

Farrow ate half his first taco in one bite, then dabbed at his lips with a napkin. "So, Alper," he said, "what do you want to see me about?"

"Got some more guys for your posse," Alper said, signaling over Farrow's shoulder to a pair of identical twenty-two-year-old twins who looked like they'd be at home blitzing quarterbacks for the local university. Both had blond crew cuts, blue eyes and bodies that paid tribute to weight training and the influence of steroids. They got up from the table they were sitting at and brought over their trays, which were loaded with enough fast food for an entire backfield.

"Ned, this is B.L. and Kenny Simms," Alper said, handling introductions. "Old friends of Mr. B."

Farrow shook the brothers' hands, taking care to put his full strength into each handshake. "I know you guys," he said. There was a trace of smugness in his voice. "ARC, right?"

"Yeah, that's us," B.L. said.

"Nice little job you did on those shines last month," Farrow told them.

"Piece of cake," B.L. boasted nonchalantly.

"What's the B.L. stand for?"

"Not Bruce Lee," B.L. snorted as he dragged a handful of french fries through a mound of catsup, then stuffed them in his mouth.

Alper laid out the plan he had in mind. "For the time being, we want ARC to keep a low profile. Nothing out in the open, nothing to draw attention to themselves. But we figure that doesn't mean they can't be out on their own, maybe keeping an eye open for this Hobbs kid."

"Sounds fine with me," Farrow said. He looked at the twins. "I could use some coverage up Rancho Drive around the North Vegas Airport and down around Tropicana Wash and Boulder Junction. Think you can handle it?"

B.L. shrugged. "Sure, man. Suppose we find him. What then?"

Farrow pulled a business card from his shirt and scribbled some numbers on the back before handing it over. "You see him, give me a call and keep him in your sights."

"How about if we just take care of him?"

"No go," Alper said. "It's got to be taken care of through Farrow, or at least through the cops."

"Why?" Kenny Simms asked between bites of his double fish fillet.

"There are other noses poking around in this business, that's why," Alper reminded the twins. "It's not good enough just to have him iced. It has to have legit written all over it. Last thing we need is for ARC to be tied up with it. Understand?"

Kenny Simms made a face. His brother leaned forward, shifting his gaze back and forth between Alper and Farrow as he talked. "Look, I know about these other men—Able Team. We got a score to settle with them. We'll help you get Hobbs, but he's nothing to us. You gotta let me and Kenny have the Team."

"First things first, okay?" Alper had finished his chili dog and he reached over to pilfer another one from B.L.'s tray. "Okay?"

"Okay," B.L. murmured.

"Good, then get cracking."

The twins got up from the table, scooping what was left of their lunch into a Ford pickup parked in front of the hot dog stand. Farrow watched them drive off, then turned to Alper. "What's this about them having a score to settle with Able Team?"

"Their sister handled a lot of the porno action this side of the Mississippi," Alper revealed. "Claudette Simms. Got herself killed up in Wyoming when Able Team raided the ranch she was using for film shoots."

"I think I remember that."

Alper took a sip from his Coke, then went on, "One of the reasons they started up this whole skinhead thing was because Able Team went up against the original ARC back in New York and New Orleans at one point. They figured once word got around, the Team might end up here, falling into a trap."

"Hmm." Farrow finished his lunch and lighted a cigarette. "Guess maybe they aren't as dumb as they look, after all."

"You're right on that count," Alper agreed. "And listen, another thing. I know Burlington hired you on this one, but we figure things will wash better if you're officially contracted through Kennesey. Global's still clean, so there'll be fewer questions if you're the one who gets Hobbs."

"Not *if*, Alper," Farrow promised. *"When..."*

BACK AT THE DROMEDARY, Gadgets Schwarz fixed a scrambler to his room phone and went through the familiar and meticulous series of diversionary tactics that ensured his call to Stony Man Farm could be neither traced or taped. His call was answered by Aaron Kurtzman, the Farm's resident communications expert and the only man Schwarz bowed to when it came to knowledge of the specialized world of electronics and computers. The Bear, so nicknamed because of a hulking physique that had been only partially compromised by a bullet-caused paralysis below the waist, seemed to be in good spirits.

"Things are moving along on the gymnasium," he reported. "Plans are approved, materials on order, and we've got a crew lined up to come in and get the sucker built once the ground out here thaws a little."

"Sounds great, Bear."

"But I assume you're calling about more than that."

"Right. Need you to pitch in and do a little snooping around for us," Schwarz said, glancing at notes he'd prepared prior to patching through to the Farm. "The cops out here are trying to be helpful, but they only go so far and so fast, and none of the Bureau people are in town to help grease the skids. We want to cut a few corners."

"Just let me know what you need and I'll get on it," Kurtzman said.

Schwarz knew it was no idle boast. It had taken thousands of hours and millions of dollars, but over the years Aaron Kurtzman had pieced together a custom-made intelligence gathering system at Stony Man Farm that easily rivaled that of any bigger agency operating out of Washington. Whether it was tapping into Department of Motor Vehicles files to match license plates with vehicle owners, or pulling rap sheets from interstate FBI computer data banks, or even more adventurous taps into the top-security dossiers of other high-ranking law enforcement agencies, Bear knew the path of least resistance. It was a path that would give him the material he sought without leaving any trace of the means by which he'd performed his technological wizardry.

"For starters," Schwarz said, "the robbery they want to pin on Hobbs went down at a warehouse for some outfit called Global Imports. I talked to some of their people and they seem to be on the level, just your basic retail outlet. But it might be worth running a deeper check on, okay?"

"No problem."

After Gadgets had passed along all the info he had on Global, he switched focus. "Next, try to drag up Vinnie Hobbs's file and see if you can find someone who might have a reason to give him or his family a problem. If you come up with anything to do with guns or burglary, flag it and go deeper."

"Fine, but you know that with that newspaper job he's probably stepped on a lot of toes," Kurtzman said. "I remember the last time he wrote he even said he'd done a few big exposés on the Mob."

"Exactly," Schwarz said. "We're figuring they have to fit in here somewhere, maybe with both this Hobbs thing and the business with ARC. Small town like this, could be we'll turn up the same people."

"Wouldn't surprise me a bit. Anything else?"

"Yeah, one more thing. Just to be on the safe side, do a run on Billy Hobbs, too. I'm sure that what Vinnie's told us is on the mark, but..." Schwarz's voice trailed off suddenly and he pulled his ear away from the phone receiver. He could hear a faint sound just outside his door.

"Gadgets? You still there?"

"I'll call you back, Bear."

Schwarz quietly set the phone down on the bed beside him and pulled his Government Model from his shoulder holster. With silent, catlike grace he pounced across the carpet to the door. There was a peephole in the wood and he peered through it, spotting what appeared to be a maid getting ready to unlock Lyons's room next door.

Keeping his gun out of view but at the ready, Schwarz opened his door, startling the maid, an older woman wearing a rust-colored uniform.

"Excuse me," he told her, "but we specifically asked not to have our rooms tended to until we checked out."

The woman eyed Schwarz nervously, still somewhat shaken by his abrupt appearance. "I...they didn't tell me. I just got back from vacation."

"Well, check with your people and leave things alone here, okay?"

The woman nodded and slowly wheeled her cart down the corridor to a room that had a Please Service tag dangling from the doorknob. She let herself in and closed the door behind. Schwarz closed his door and used the phone to call the main desk. The maid's story checked out.

A few minutes later, as Schwarz was trying to get back in touch with the Farm, there was a knock on the door. It was Lyons, and he didn't look too pleased with the way things were going.

"I spent all morning hassling with those Vegas Keystone Kops," he groused. "I don't know whether they're deliberately incompetent or what, but it's like slogging through mud to get anywhere with them. I say we just do without them, even if it means covering some of the same ground."

"Sounds fair to me," Schwarz said. "I got through to Bear and he'll take the high road. That leaves us with the low..."

NED FARROW WAS DRIVING slowly past the glitter palaces on Fremont Street when he suddenly goosed the accelerator and veered around a cab double-parked in front of the Showboat. A woman who looked to be wearing little more than an oversize sweater and fishnet stockings heard the screech of his tires and blanched at the sight of Farrow's Mustang swinging back toward the curb. She had just struck up a conversation with a tongue-tied conventioneer from Idaho, looking for thrills he couldn't find back home.

"Sorry, honey, but maybe another time," she told the bespectacled would-be john. "I just remembered I got some other business to attend to."

She turned and started down the nearest side street, hoping to avoid Farrow, but he followed her, slowing his Mustang as he kept an eye on her.

"Not like you to play hard to get, Annie doll."

"I'm in a hurry," she said, refusing to meet the man's gaze.

"Then maybe you ought to hop in and let me take you wherever you're going."

"No thanks."

Annie lengthened her stride and was about to duck into a drugstore when Farrow suddenly guided his convertible up over the curb, nearly running her over. She let out an involuntary gasp and reeled backward a few steps, staring at Farrow with a mixture of fear and anger.

"I wasn't asking, sweet cakes," the bounty hunter told her, leaning across the front seat and opening the passenger's door. "Get in."

Annie glanced around. There were several tourists a few storefronts away, but none of them seemed too anxious to get involved in her dilemma. She knew that by going into the drugstore she'd only be postponing the inevitable, so she sighed and reluctantly got into the Mustang with Farrow.

"That a girl," Farrow told her as he backed off the sidewalk. "I knew you had some sense."

Annie stared straight ahead as Farrow shifted gears and continued down the side street. "What do you want?" she asked coldly.

"Hey, is that any way to talk to your benefactor?" Farrow asked. "Or maybe all this streetwalking's affected your memory. Remember last week, when you were cornered over by the Lady Luck by that pervert with the chunk of hose?"

"Yes, I remember," she muttered.

"Oh, good," Farrow said. He turned his Mustang down a side alley and activated his customized top, which began to whir up from behind the back seat. "Then maybe you remember saying you owed me one for that."

Annie took a deep breath and forced a smile, turning to the man in the Stetson. "You're right," she whispered huskily, trailing her left hand past the gearshift and touching Farrow's thigh. "Sorry. It's just that I've been having a bad day."

"Me, too," Farrow said, pulling into a parking structure and heading for the upper levels. Staying in low gear, he took his right hand off the shift knob and placed it on Annie's hand, guiding hers up from his thigh. "Maybe we'll both feel a lot better if we get some of the tension out of our system, don't you think?"

"Fine with me," Annie said, trying to mask the resignation in her voice as she went along with Farrow. It was bad enough that she had to hustle tricks for a living. Passing out freebies didn't have much appeal to her, even if she did feel a debt to Farrow for having rescued her from the sadist at the Lady Luck.

Five levels up there were few cars in the parking structure. Farrow pulled off to a far corner and parked, shutting off the engine. He adjusted his seat, easing it back slightly. "Okay, Annie, get my gun."

The woman moved closer, when something resting on the dashboard caught her eye. It was a photo of Billy Hobbs.

"You looking for him?" she asked.

Farrow's mood changed almost instantaneously. "You seen him?" he demanded.

"Maybe," the woman said, recalling the man she'd taken the wallet from earlier that morning.

Farrow reached out and grabbed Annie's hair, giving it a sharp tug. She winced as she felt her head being turned sharply around so that she faced him. "Maybe nothing," he said sharply, no longer interested in quick sex. "Where is he?"

7

"Reminds me a little of my old home turf," Blancanales said as he stared out at the passing view of a poor,
largely Hispanic neighborhood in North Las Vegas.
Old three-story apartment complexes huddled close
together along the street, most of them in a state of
disrepair. In several of the small, cramped yards,
women were out trying to supervise their children as
they hung wet clothes out to dry, even though the temperature hovered just above fifty degrees and the wind
made it feel even colder. Some of the children were
gathered near a cyclone fence, watching three men
working on the engine of a run-down Ford station
wagon parked along the curb.

"Yeah, once you get off the Strip, you find out this
city's not that much different from any other," Vincent Hobbs explained as he brought his Chevette to a
stop at a red light on Bonanza and flicked on his turn
signal. "It takes a lot of people to accommodate the
tourist traffic, and most of them don't make that much
money. Most folks aren't going to bother tipping maid
service a dollar when that means passing up four yanks
on the quarter slots, know what I mean?"

"Yeah, afraid so."

The light changed and Hobbs continued, giving Pol a tour of the areas that had been most recently targeted for ARC activity. He'd covered some of the incidents for the *Herald* and was going around with Blancanales, not only to help Able Team on their official mission, but also to see if he could come up with some new information or fresh perspective on his story of racial intolerance in the gambling capital.

Five blocks down the road he pulled into an unused parking lot adjacent to a ravaged building that was charred from the effects of a recent fire. Hobbs explained, "This was the liquor distributorship that was bombed. Happened around eleven at night, probably when ARC didn't think anyone would be in. Set off a C-4 explosive here in front and threw a Molotov cocktail through a back window into the room where all the stock was kept. Torch that much booze and you get a blast as potent as dynamite.

"The saddest thing is, there were people inside doing inventory when it all came down. Poor guys never had a chance."

Blancanales shook his head in disgust. "I think you're being generous when you say ARC didn't know there were people in there. Remember, we dealt with them, and they had no qualms about killing. Hell, if they had pulled off that scheme of dumping nuke waste into the New York water system, who's to say where the death toll would have stopped."

"Maybe you're right," Hobbs said as he pulled out of the driveway, "but I guess it's more comforting to think these young kids are just ignorant and not malicious."

"It might be more comforting, but my money says you're dreaming."

Hobbs sighed. "I just can't figure what's gotten into kids these days."

"Rough world out there," Blancanales suggested. "Sometimes it seems easier to deal with if you start painting things black and white. Of course, when you do that, you're just asking for trouble."

Back on Bonanza, Hobbs and Blancanales began to see the proliferation of homeless people wandering the sidewalks and loitering at street corners. "These folks are the new scapegoats," Hobbs said. "And it isn't just ARC going after them, because a lot of them are white. We get reports that sometimes the college frats bring out pledges to beat up people as part of their initiation. Once a couple of guys on the football team got suspended when they got caught doing it, and they said they were just out for kicks and trying to work off a little agression."

"Madre de Dios," Pol cursed under his breath, feeling his heart jog with the anger building up inside him. He was already formulating one possible plan of attack for getting to ARC, and there was a part of him that loved the prospect of going undercover. Dress down to pass as a transient and wait for a gang of cowards to come up on him, then let them find out what it was like to get the living crap beaten out of them.

Farther down the street, Hobbs pulled into a parking spot in front of the North Las Vegas Rescue Mission, a dilapidated cinder-block building with a roof of corrugated steel. Out in front of the building a thirty-year-old woman in a plain brown dress was watching as five men with paintbrushes applied a fresh coat of white paint to the building's facade, which had been spray-painted with several derogatory messages. Pol could still make out one of them: Scum served here.

Pol and Hobbs got out of the car and walked over to the woman, who turned her back on the painters to greet them. Pol felt his anger washing away as he took a good look at her. Short and thin, she nonetheless projected an abundance of inner strength and self-confidence. Her dark hair was pulled back in a ponytail, which emphasized her clear, dark complexion. Recognizing Hobbs, she parted her rounded lips into a faint smile that vaguely reminded Pol of his sister. The vague stirring inside him went far beyond a sibling sort of attraction, however.

"Hi, Donna," Vincent said.

"Hello, Vince," the woman responded in a warm, resonant voice.

"This is my old friend Rosario Blancanales," Vincent said, indicating Pol.

"Pol," Blancanales told Donna. "Please, call me Pol."

"Pol," Vincent went on, "this is Donna Alvarez. She runs the mission here. We met a few months ago when I was doing a series of stories on her work with the homeless."

"And about the way they were being treated," Donna added, her smile fading momentarily as she gestured behind her.

"It's terrible," Hobbs said, staring at the slogan. "When did it happen?"

"Couple of nights ago. You can't believe how much begging I had to do just to get someone to donate paint and brushes. Anyway," she said, turning back to Blancanales and offering her hand, "it's a pleasure to meet you, Pol. I can't say as I've come across that name before."

"Short for Politician," Blancanales explained. "Nickname. I didn't care much for having Rosario shortened to Rosie."

All three of them laughed, then Donna turned to Vincent. "I wish I had some good news for you, but I've asked around about your nephew and no one here has seen him. We'll keep an eye open still, of course."

"Thanks, I appreciate it," Hobbs said. "I'm just on my way to work, but Pol wanted to spend a little time around here, just to get a feel for what's happening."

"Oh, fine," Donna said. She asked Blancanales, "You're a politician, then?"

"No, not really," Pol said. "I'm a . . . well, I guess you could say I do some social work."

"Wonderful!" Donna said. "That's something we can always use more of in this town. Look, I think these guys have a handle on the painting here. How about if I give you a look around inside and we can talk, okay?"

Pol nodded. "That'd be great." Glancing over Donna's shoulder, he saw Hobbs raise an eyebrow suggestively. It was a wasted gesture, though. Pol didn't need anyone else to tell him that there was some serious chemistry going on here.

GADGETS SCHWARZ'S PARANOIA over the incident with the maid had gotten the better of him, and when he and Lyons showed up at Fremont Trailer Home, they had brought their belongings with them, having checked out of the Dromedary Hotel. Vincent Hobbs had extended an open invitation for Able Team to stay at his trailer and they'd decided to take him up on it, figuring that it would put them in the best position to be around if Billy should call again. A secondary reason, which hadn't been discussed openly but was tacitly acknowledged by all parties, was that the Team was concerned that any trouble that had come Billy's way might very well find its way back to the trailer, and they wanted to do what they could to protect their friend. Of course, the chance to once again sample some of Vinnie's near-legendary meals had also been a factor.

In addition to a second bedroom, which had been used by Billy prior to his disappearance, Vincent also had an enclosed porch added on to his trailer, complete with a Franklin furnace capable of warding off any chill in the air. There was a couch long enough to serve as a bed and an old army cot in the closet, giving each man a place to sleep. It would be crowded, but Lyons and Schwarz suspected they wouldn't have to put up with it for more than a week. From previous experience, they knew that their way of doing things tended to produce results in a fraction of the time that more conspicuous agencies and their attendant bureaucracies could.

As they set out their gear in the extension room, Lyons paused to take a look at Vinnie Hobbs's gun collection, which was displayed behind glass in a case mounted to the east wall. The Ingram Model 10 submachine gun was inoperable, as demanded by law for private owners, but it still looked every bit the deadly compact weapon that it was. An M-14 dating back to Hobbs's Vietnam days was mounted with its bayonet fixed to the barrel and an empty magazine suspended perpendicular to the stock at a point several inches in front of the trigger. An unattached M-203 grenade launcher hung at an angle that showed off the nicks and gashes it had taken during the infamous siege of Stony Man Farm several years ago, when Vincent Hobbs had been forced to forsake his spatula and gardening trowel in favor of a weapon more apt to repel the infiltrators. It was the M-203 that had deflected bullets that would otherwise have added Hobbs to the casualty list, and even though it was no longer usable, its sentimental value was significant.

"Bet the neighbors would shit if they saw all this," Lyons said as he looked the weapons over.

"Not as much as they would if they knew how much more we brought along with us," Schwarz said, patting the .45 tucked in his shoulder holster.

"Well, most of them saw us flashing our popguns at that Yanders dude the other night, remember?" Lyons said. "With any luck, they'll be wary enough to stay out of our way."

"Except when we want to ask some questions," Schwarz corrected, going over to the gun case and tapping the glass near a vacant space in the display. "I don't know what kind of job the cops did of sniffing around here for witnesses, but it seems to me that somebody might have seen something out of the ordinary the day that Cobra was swiped from here."

"Like I told you back at the hotel," Lyons complained, "I got nowhere trying to find out what the cops had on this. The officers who answered the call weren't in and they were a week and a half behind on their paperwork, so all I could get was secondhand info. I'm not sure, but I think that the only witness they came up with was that Yanders fella's wife.''

"The one we saved from being diced?" Schwarz said.

"I think so."

"Well," Schwarz said, slipping a coat over his shoulder holster, "I guess we might as well make that square one."

"After that big whoop-de-do with her old man, could be she's not there," Lyons said. "I mean, unless they hauled him in, she's just wifebait waiting for another beating."

"One way to find out," Schwarz said. "How about I go check it out while you patch in to the Farm and let 'em know we're staying here."

Lyons nodded, adding, "If the Axman cometh, be sure to give a holler."

"Will do."

Schwarz left Hobbs's trailer and circled around their rental minivan to the Yanderses' residence. Leila Yanders was outside with a repairman who was giving her an estimate on fixing the trailer side where her husband had gotten carried away with his ax. She looked much better than she had the other night, and when she spotted Schwarz she gave him a slight wave of recognition. Gadgets waited until she was through with the repairman, then crossed the trampled lawn to join her.

"Afternoon, ma'am."

"I want to thank you again for your help with Richard," the woman said. "I was so afraid it was going to end up terribly."

"Didn't seem to me it was really that much of a happy ending, but you're welcome."

"Oh, but it was," she stammered. "Or at least I hope it will end up that way. You see, my husband's been depressed and drinking way too much since he got laid off work a couple of months ago. I kept trying to get him to take a long hard look at himself, but I guess he just had to hit rock bottom before he decided enough was enough. He's at a rehabilitation center now. I just saw him for lunch and already he seems better. So, you see, it turned out to be a blessing in disguise."

"I'm glad it's working out," Schwarz said. "Listen, I was wondering if I could ask you a few questions about your neighbor, Mr. Hobbs. We're friends of his and we're looking into that burglary of his house."

Like all members of Able Team, Gadgets had a badge and ID card for such situations, showing him to be a special federal agent. He showed the identification to the woman.

"Well, after what you did to help, I naturally trust you," Leila said, "but, you see, I'm late for work right now, so I really can't talk. Did you check with the police? They took a report of that man I saw behind Mr. Hobbs's place."

"Man?"

"Yes," Leila said as she headed for her Ford Escort, parked under a carport next to the trailer. "There was a meter man there the same day as that burglary. It stuck in my mind because the regular guy had been by earlier in the week. I asked this other fella what he was doing and he said someone had reported a gas leak and they were trying to trace it."

"So do you remember what he looked like?" Schwarz asked as Leila got in and started her car.

Leila nodded. "Yes, but can you check with the police? I gave them a full description and they did up a composite with one of those IdentiKits of theirs. Sorry, but I really do have to go."

Schwarz thanked the woman and waited until she pulled out of the driveway, then crossed back to Hobbs's trailer. When he went inside, he found Lyons sitting near the phone, staring into space.

"Problem?"

"Maybe so," Lyons said. "I just talked with Bear back at the Farm. From what he was able to dig up on Global Imports, they're clean. Very upscale operation, deal mostly with Persian rugs and pricey things from the Middle East. According to the insurance claim they filed, they lost more than half a million in rugs in that robbery the other night."

Schwarz whistled. "That's a pretty penny, especially in a town like this. But where's the problem?"

"Well, apparently Global's pretty upset about the heist...the guard that was killed had been with them for a long time, and they want to make sure that whoever was behind it gets caught. So they've posted a reward and they've also brought in a bounty hunter."

"Bounty hunter? You're kidding."

Lyons shook his head. "Guy by the name of Ned Farrow. Ex-cop out of Carson City, been working Vegas two, three years now. Showy guy, but he's clean, too. Only rap on him is that he tends to be trigger-happy. Watched too much Steve McQueen in *Wanted: Dead or Alive*, I guess."

"Great," Schwarz said, dropping into an easy chair across from Lyons. "If he gets to Billy before we do, that poor kid's going to be in some deep shit."

8

The old packing plant was a veritable labyrinth of side rooms, nooks and crannies. Stripped of salvageable equipment and abandoned less than three years ago, its subsequent deterioration had been swift and pronounced. It had been aided by a combination of Las Vegas's brutal weather cycles, the destructive instincts of teenage vandals eager to find an outlet for their frustrations in a town that offered little to those not old enough to gamble and the indifference of transients who used the rotting shell as a periodic refuge. The stink of urine, vomit and excrement was all-pervading and overpowering, and although his stomach growled for attention, Billy Hobbs was too nauseated to try to satisfy his hunger. Crouched back in a far corner up on the second floor, he shuddered to think how rank the air in the building must get in the summer with the blistering midday sun beating down on it.

He'd fallen asleep at one point, after dragging himself into the plant and crawling up the steps to get away from those few snoring souls bedded down on the ground floor. Now that he was awake again, Billy leaned to one side and peered out through the shattered window to his left, trying to judge the time by how far the sun had traveled. It was late in the afternoon, he guessed. He stayed put, still exhausted and racked with pain from his earlier fall. Fortunately all of his cuts had been shallow; the bleeding had soon stopped. When he pressed against some of his ribs the pain was sharp, but not as excruciating as earlier. With any luck they were just bruised.

Luck.

What a laugh, he thought bitterly, tears rimming his eyes. He'd been born under a bad sign—The Billy Hobbs Story, a tragedy. Billy looked up at the paint-flaked ceiling and laughed lightly to himself. Yeah, Billy, you're out of a regular Russian novel, just like the ones you read in the prison library. Charlie Sheen could play you in the movie, maybe find some sort of nobility in all this suffering...nah, forget it. Who'd want to pay to watch a loser like Billy Hobbs? If anything, the world would rather turn its collective head and look the other way. Overwhelmed by misery, Billy's near-giddy laughter turned to a soft, quiet sobbing.

An hour passed, then he heard voices downstairs—three, maybe four transients talking to one another between the long, loud yawns with which they tried to shake off the fatigue that was the constant adversary of the homeless.

"Best be headin' over to the mission to get in line for some supper."

"Yeah, guess yer right there. I jus' wish they'd give you the food and that'd be it, y'know? None of that preachin' shit."

"Amen, bro. I get somethin' in my belly and it's Jesus this and Jesus that until I get indigestion."

"We could panhandle up on Fremont, work up a little stake for one of them buffets."

"Ah, screw that. They don't hand out for shit no more. People up there are in too goddamn much of a hurry to throw their money down some damn machine. They won't think about giving it to us."

"How about if we all get together, y'know, and case some guy out. Y'know, follow 'im to some alley and let 'im have it."

"Too risky. Cops catch you at that and you get whacked with a billy club till your bones are all broken and your brains are scrambled. Remember what they did to Johnny Slim out behind the Fremont? No thank you. I'll take the mission and just plug my ears for the preachin'."

The men continued talking as they walked out of the building, then closed a door behind them. In the sudden silence, Billy felt a cold shudder. Those men had sounded so pathetic, so hopeless, and they were spelling out the kind of life Billy had to look forward to. Forget those dreams of hopping a train to a new life. Stupid romantic hokum. Nothing noble about hoboes these days. It's the lot of losers, Billy boy, he chided himself, and it's where you're going to end up the way things are going.

"What am I going to do?" he asked himself.

He was startled by the sound of his voice, strained and feeble, echoing off the naked walls of this cubicle that had become his home. Did he really think he could last long here, choking on the stench, cringing from the law? What kind of life was that?

No, there had to be another way.

He longed to find a phone and call his uncle again, beg for some help and understanding. Uncle Vince would listen, would come to his aid. Hell, why hadn't he followed his uncle's advice the first time instead of staying out and trying to jump that train? Maybe Uncle Vince was right. If he was innocent, he shouldn't have anything to fear. A lawyer could look out for his rights, make sure that the right evidence was found to nail the bastards that framed him.

"Phone," he whispered, as if mouthing the word would help muster the strength needed to go and find one. He still had some change in his pocket. He could do what was right, force his luck to change.

Inching across the floor, taking care to avoid shards of fallen glass, Billy placed himself in the sunlight pouring through the window. The warmth felt comforting, reassuring. He'd just lie there a while longer, see if the heat might take some of the stiffness out of his limbs.

Several minutes passed, then Billy heard the main door to the packing plant creak open downstairs. Then footsteps. Slow, certain steps, deliberately quiet.

Too quiet.

Billy sat up, no longer paying attention to his pain. Some deeper instinct commanded him, put him immediately on his guard. On his hands and knees, he crept across the floor, past the rusting remains of a toppled water cooler. From the doorway he had a partially obstructed view of the main room downstairs, which was dominated by huge presses and other obsolete machinery that had been left behind when the plant closed down. Sunlight pouring through the opened door cast the shadow of a man on one of the presses, and Billy could see that the man was carrying a gun.

"Billy," a voice suddenly called out. "Billy Hobbs!"

Billy shrank back from the doorway, terror in his eyes. This couldn't be happening. He froze in place, holding his breath, but his heart pounded so fiercely between his ribs that he was afraid the man below was going to be able to hear the palpitations.

"I know you're in here somewhere," Ned Farrow called out calmly, walking with less restraint now.

Billy was able to tell where the man was even though he could no longer see his shadow. From the sounds below, Farrow was methodically searching the ground floor, pausing outside any doorway, then lunging in, only to withdraw moments later. There were several muttered curses Billy couldn't make out, before Farrow called out again. "I'm taking you in dead or alive, Billy. The choice is up to you."

A fresh wave of fear washed through Billy. He drew in a deep breath and held it, tensing every fiber of his being, trying his best not to move.

"Okay, I guess you must be upstairs, hmm?"

There was an unmistakable sound of footsteps on the metal grating of the main staircase.

Billy slowly rose to his feet, looking around the room. Even if he could squirm through a broken section of the window, it was a twenty-foot drop to the concrete below. There was no way he could make it.

Now he could hear Farrow leaving the steps and starting down the walkway that ran past all the second-story rooms. He followed the same ritual as downstairs, pausing outside the door, then lunging into the opening. Getting closer each time.

"I'm getting impatient, Billy."

Billy looked down at the cooler stand. It was his only chance. He let his breath out slowly as he quietly and cautiously straddled the stand.

Farrow was only a couple of rooms away now.

Billy leaned over, closed his fingers around the legs of the stand. When he took a closer look at the overturned cooler, a gasp nearly leaped from his lips. In the shadows of the stand, only a few inches away, two large brown rats were circling inside what used to be a refrigerated compartment. One of them sprang up the walls of the compartment and paused, tail twitching up against Billy's right hand. It was all Billy could do to fight off his revulsion and concentrate on the greater threat outside the door. The rat fidgeted in place, still trying to make sense of the giant that had rousted its lair.

Billy tensed when he saw Farrow's shadow stretch across the doorway. Bracing himself, he waited until he thought the other man was going to make his move, then let out an inhuman shriek and made his own countermove. Hoisting the cooler stand, he charged for the doorway, rats leaping to the floor as he collided headlong with Ned Farrow, knocking the bounty hunter off balance.

The Casull exploded in the close quarters with a sound like concentrated thunder, but fortunately for Billy the stand deflected the brunt of the .454 slug blasting out of the gun's lethal barrel. Still, he felt a hot stinging sensation as shrapnel drove itself into his shoulder and upper chest.

Carried along by his own momentum, Billy managed to bowl Farrow back out into the walkway, where they both bounded against the railing, nearly toppling over it.

"Son of a bitch!" Farrow raged as the corner of the rusty stand ripped a long gash just above his left eye, obscuring his vision with a shower of his own blood. When he hit the railing, taking most of the blow against his right hip, he had to drop his gun to fight for his balance. The Casull clattered to the walkway and was inadvertently kicked over the side as the two men grappled with each other.

Billy Hobbs was out of his mind with fear and fought like a man possessed. His pummeling blows were largely wasted in their reckless fury, but he connected with enough hits to force Farrow to stagger backward to the staircase. He tumbled down the first flight to an eight-foot-square landing, where he lay sprawled in a momentary daze. Billy raced down after him, not concerned so much with finishing off the fight as with getting away before Farrow recovered. Once he reached the ground floor, Billy briefly looked for the Casull, but it had fallen into one of the larger pieces of machinery and there was no way he was going to take the time to try to find it. Instead he stumbled, fell, fought back to his feet and reeled out the door through which Farrow had entered the plant. He ran with all his might, the once-vague sensation of pain in his shoulders and upper chest growing in intensity. But even when he glanced down long enough to see how severely he was bleeding from his newest wounds, he refused to slow down and try to stanch the flow. He turned his gaze on a patch of mesquite fifty yards ahead and, beyond that, the hopeful sanctuary of North Las Vegas. If he could only get that far...

9

"Hey, it's no problem, really," Pol told Donna Alvarez as he grabbed the wax-layered cardboard box filled with old produce from the Val-U Supermart on Michael Way, half a mile from the mission.

"I don't know," the woman said apologetically, "I feel like I've drafted you into involuntary servitude."

"Trust me," Pol told her with a grin, "We Blancanaleses don't do anything we don't want to. Look, your regular driver's sick, I'm available and I'm glad to help out. End of discussion, okay?"

Donna smiled. "Okay."

Pol carried the produce out to the mission's truck, an old rattletrap donated by the Postal Service after it had put in its regulation number of miles. The traditional post office blue had been painted over with a pale yellow and stenciled with the name of the mission and a phone number people could call if they wished to donate food or supplies to the ongoing effort to assist the homeless of Las Vegas.

"We've gotten a reasonably good response from the community," Donna said as she held the back doors of the truck open so Pol could load the produce inside.

"That's the understatement of the week," Pol said, setting the carton next to the other provisions they'd picked up earlier. There were two-day-old bakery goods from a Freshbake outlet store on Decatur, flats of expired and dented canned soup from the Nature's Best plant on Lake Mead Boulevard and irregular paper plates and plastic eating utensils from Miller Wholesale Inc. over on West Washington.

"You wouldn't believe all the red tape and lobbying we had to go through to be able to get some of these things," Donna said as they got back in the truck and headed back to the mission. "FDA agencies, Health Department, you name it. I mean, even though all this stuff is perfectly safe and edible, most of the laws say it has to go in the trash after x number of days."

"Good old bureaucracy." Pol laughed gently. "It helps make the world go round."

"And round and round in circles," Donna added. "I swear, sometimes I think these stuffed shirts think people were made to serve the law instead of vice versa."

"In my line of business I run into that all the time," Blancanales said, turning east on Washington and driving past the Las Vegas Golf Club. The sight of the idle rich chasing white balls across landscaped fairways was somewhat jarring in contrast to the glimpses of abject poverty he'd seen while making the errand runs with Donna. "And the real problems come when decent people abide by those laws and find themselves at the mercy of those who play by their own set of rules."

"I have to say, Pol, you've been pretty evasive about this 'social work' you do," Donna commented. "What are you holding back?"

"What do you mean?"

"I like you, and I have a good feeling about you," she confided, "but I just don't think either you or Vincent have been fully on the level with me."

"Oh?" As he idled at a light, Pol glanced over at Donna. "What makes you say that?"

"Well, for starters, there's that bulge under your coat I'm not supposed to be able to notice," Donna said. "I don't know that many social workers who carry guns around on them."

Pol didn't respond immediately. The light changed and he turned down Tonopah Drive, which intersected with Bonanza a block farther on. "You don't miss a trick, do you?" he finally told Donna.

"Not if I can help it," Donna said. "Tell me, Pol, who are you really?"

Pol sighed. She had a right to know. "I'm a special agent of sorts with the government," he explained as he drove. "I'm trying to help Vinnie out with this problem with his nephew, and there's a few angles that need looking into. One of them has to do with the Aryan Right Coalition. You're familiar with them, I trust."

Donna nodded. "Of course. They're probably the ones who put that obscene graffiti on the front of the mission, and I know they were behind that liquor store bombing the other week."

"Our thinking is that these kids aren't acting solely on their own," Blancanales speculated. "Vinnie and a few other people figure that some heavy players are behind them."

"Like the Mob, for instance," Donna said matter-of-factly. "I have no doubt that's the case."

Pol pulled into the driveway next to the mission and drove around to the back, parking as close to the rear entrance as possible. As he turned off the engine, he told Donna, "We want to put them out of circulation as quickly and effectively as possible."

"ARC or the Mob?" Donna asked.

"Both," Pol said.

"I think we should talk some more about this," Donna said. "But first let's get this stuff unloaded."

They got out of the truck and were joined by several homeless men putting in volunteer work at the mission. The goods in the back of the truck were unloaded and carried into the large kitchen, where more volunteers were already starting to put together the offerings that would be served up when the food lines gathered later that afternoon. Once the task was finished, Donna asked Pol, "I assume you like a good burrito."

"Yeah, sure."

"Good. I want to take you to Pedro's down on Maryland Avenue. Best food in town."

"Fine by me."

Donna told another of the mission employees that she was taking a break, then led Pol to her small Opel in the parking lot.

As the two of them got in and drove off, one of the men who had helped unload the supplies wandered away from the mission and put a quarter into a corner phone. He dialed a number, then glanced furtively around him, making sure no one was within earshot. When he got an answer on the other line, he said, "They're just leaving now. Going to Pedro's..."

NED FARROW STARED bitterly at the splint bound to his left wrist with a tightly wrapped length of gauze. Despite the painkillers he'd been given, he could still feel a faint stabbing sensation if he moved the fingers too much.

"Shit," he muttered, shifting in his hospital bed.

"Well, it could have been worse. It could have been your gun hand," Wes Burlington said. The thin man was sitting in a chair next to the bed.

"Yeah, how about that." Farrow didn't seem too consoled by Burlington's remark. His skirmish with Billy Hobbs had also left him with more than thirty stitches on his face where the cooler stand had struck him, and both eyes were bruised and swollen partially shut. The pain and discomfort of his wounds, however, paled next to the blow his pride had suffered.

"Little runt squirmed off the hook," he seethed quietly. "Again."

"You said you hit him with one shot at close range," Burlington reminded Farrow. "I know about the Casull. With that, there's no such thing as flesh wounds. I don't think he'll be going very far on us."

"Well, if somebody else gets to him first, I want him kept alive," Farrow demanded. "Anybody turns off his light, it's gonna be me."

"We'll see," Burlington said calmly.

"See nothing!" Farrow snapped. "I got dibs on that kid!"

The older man got up from his chair and walked over to the door, closing it so their conversation wouldn't drift out into the hallway. When he returned to Farrow's bed, he eyed the bounty hunter firmly. "I'm sorry, Ned, but it doesn't work that way. You know better. In an organization like ours, we always have to keep the big picture in mind. Personal matters go in the back seat. Understood?''

''Yeah, well I'm not your organization, Mr. B.,'' Farrow reminded him. ''I'm free-lance.''

''For what I'm paying you, I expect a little loyalty,'' Burlington countered. ''And don't try to tell me you aren't looking to join ranks once we've built up our power base.''

The two men faced off quietly a moment, their features falling into that same emotionless state that served them so well at the poker game. Farrow was the first to break the silence. ''Okay, we play it your way. But if that Hobbs kid is still on the loose once I'm out of here, I'm going back after him. My terms.''

''That's acceptable,'' Burlington conceded. He sat back down. ''In the meantime, we're a little concerned about this Able Team. One of them, the Hispanic fellow, has been hanging out with Donna Alvarez all day. We're concerned that he might have been posted as her bodyguard. If the other witnesses get protection, too, a new trial's not going to look so good for Bobby.''

''Then maybe you should think about taking action before they get too entrenched,'' Farrow suggested.

''Calno's already working on it. He's got his people shadowing the Alvarez woman, and the Simms twins are on standby now that Able Team's involved. You know about the unfinished business between them.''

Farrow nodded. ''Something about their sister, right? What was her name...?''

''Claudette.''

''Yeah, right.''

"Kenny and B.L. want Blancanales as bad as you want the Hobbs boy," Burlington said.

"If that's the case," Farrow laughed, "this burg's just begun to bleed...."

PEDRO'S WAS a stylishly funky Mexican diner with outdoor tables set under a gigantic, wide-brimmed, bulb-studded sombrero that doubled as the establishment's roof and an advertising ploy tying into the razzle-dazzle of the nearby Strip. Waiters dressed like Frito Banditos tended to customers by firing trick six-guns that shot out menus that unraveled like scrolls, detailing the limited but touted fare.

"You just have to try the Borderline Burrito," Donna advised Pol, who seemed uncomfortable amid all the surrounding gimmickry.

"Okay, fine," he said.

"Make that two," Donna told the waiter, "and I'll have a large iced tea."

"Might as well make it two of those, as well," Pol said.

As the waiter rolled up the menu and tucked his toy gun back in his holster before making his way to the kitchen, Donna gestured at the crowd milling around their curbside table. "So, what do you think?"

"I think it's a mockery," Pol confessed.

"Oh, don't be so stuffy," Donna said. "This is Las Vegas, after all. And once you take your first bite, you'll change your attitude, believe me."

"We'll see," Pol said. He leaned closer to Donna. "Now, what was it you wanted to talk about?"

Donna's cheerful smile quickly gave way to a more somber look. She picked up an ashtray, also in the shape of a sombrero, and began fidgeting with it nervously as she spoke. "The reason I know the syndicate's trying to get back into Vegas is because they killed my husband last year when he refused to play along with an extortion racket they were trying to set up just down the block from here."

"I'm sorry," Pol said. "I didn't know..."

Donna's eyes glimmered briefly at the first mention of her husband, but she brought herself under control and continued. "He owned a small nightclub, one of the few where there was no gambling allowed. He wanted people to have a place they could visit to have a good time without being tempted by the slots and that whole scene. It was a big success and we got a lot of referrals through Gamblers Anonymous, some write-ups in the press. That's how I first met Vincent. I was a waitress there.

"Anyway, when my husband...Eric...when Eric first started hearing from these guys, he just sort of shrugged them off and didn't think anything more about it. Then we started having problems. Vandalism, bomb threats, people coming in deliberately looking for fights.

"Eric finally had his fill and collared these guys who kept hinting about protection. He told them he knew they were behind all the trouble and if it didn't stop he was going to go to the cops."

Tears began to roll down Donna's face and she reached for a napkin to dab her eyes. Pol reached across the table and rested his hand on her forearm. "You don't have to go through all this if—"

"I want to," she insisted, taking a deep breath. "It's important that you know.

"The night after that, while Eric was taking the trash out back, there was a car waiting for him. I was inside and heard shots. When I rushed out, the car was pulling away and I saw Eric lying on the ground, holding his stomach. I don't know how, but somehow I had the presence of mind to get a good look at the car, and I recognized one of the men in back as one of the drunks who'd disrupted the bar a couple of nights before.

"They took Eric to the hospital, but it was too late. He'd lost too much blood and there was too much organ damage. I saw him buried, then I worked with the police and got Vincent's help in going after the people responsible for what happened. All in all, there were nine arrests and we managed to get convictions for five of them, including a man named Bobby Sumur. He ran a stock brokerage just two blocks over from our nightclub, but there were rumors that he had a lot of Mob connections and was using the brokerage as a front.

"I was able to pin him by working with some federal investigators. They wired me when I went to confront him after Vincent had done some investigating and found a link between Sumur and the guy in the car who shot Eric."

There was a pause as the waiter returned with their food. The aroma steaming up from the burrito platters was tempting, but Blancanales ignored it for the moment. He asked Donna, "And what happened to the people who were convicted?"

"They're all still in jail, but they're appealing for a new trial. From what I've heard, it sounds like they might get one. If that happens, I'll have to testify all over again. I've tried to put the whole thing behind me and concentrate on this work with the mission, but there are nights when it all comes back to me and I just can't sleep.''

"Have you received any calls or any threats about testifying?" Pol asked, already suspecting the answer.

Donna nodded. "They're trying to intimidate me, but I won't back down. Before he died, I promised Eric I'd see that he was avenged, and I'll see it through even if I have to go through ten more trials."

Pol gave Donna's hand a slight squeeze and waited for her to meet his gaze, then told her, "If there's anything my friends and I can do to help, it'll be done. You can count on it."

"Thank you," she replied, summoning a slight smile. "For now, you can help by taking a bite of that burrito and admitting it's the best thing you've ever tasted this side of the border."

Pol reached for a fork and cautioned Donna, "My mother's cooking excepted, of course."

"Of course."

Blancanales carved a corner off the thick, cheese-smothered burrito and bit into it. A genuine smile came across his face as he chewed the spicy beef-and-bean mixture.

"What'd I tell you?" Donna said.

"I'm in heaven," Pol said, cutting off another portion.

Over Donna's shoulder, he had a clear view of the street, only a few short yards away from their table. A tourist bus rolled past, slowing down as the passengers inside all began snapping photos of the diner. Pol flashed a thumbs-up and widened his grin.

"Aren't you the ham." Donna chuckled.

"Hey, just giving this place my official seal of approval," Pol said. "I mean, I have to admit I had my reservations when you first started bragging about this place but—*¡Madre de Dios!*"

Blancanales suddenly lunged, grabbing Donna by the shoulders and pulling her to one side a fraction of a second before an old Chevy sedan veered over the curb and plowed into the table where they had been seated. The wooden chairs splintered on impact and the table cracked sharply in half as the burrito dinners bounced on the hood of the runaway car.

Cursing a stream of epithets in Spanish, Blancanales rolled away from Donna, ignoring the screams of the nearest patrons, and bounded to his feet, jerking out his .45 automatic.

The Chevy swung back onto the street and picked up speed as it lurched through the sparse traffic, heading for the nearest side street. Blancanales knew there was no way he could get a shot away without endangering innocent bystanders, so he started off on foot, hoping to at least keep the car in sight. The fates weren't obliging, however, and by the time he'd run halfway down the block, weaving between startled pedestrians, the Chevy was nowhere to be seen.

Disgruntled, Pol holstered his gun and hurried back to the diner, where he found Donna on her feet, looking pale but otherwise uninjured.

"Like it or not," he told her, "the war's on."

10

"Don't be ridiculous, Vince," Bari Bestel told her fiancé, "I understand. Completely."

"You're sure?" the reporter asked the woman.

They were in one of the back dressing rooms at the Royalty Hotel, Vegas's newest casino. Bari, a tall, striking brunette with clover-green eyes, was a feature singer in the Royalty's highly touted "Song and Dance" show. She'd just finished an afternoon rehearsal of a new song being added to the production, so she wasn't wearing the extravagant makeup and costuming worn during performances. All she had to do was grab her mink stole and purse and she was ready to leave. Still, she paused in the room with Vincent, placing a slender hand under his chin and looking him in the eyes.

"I love you, Vincent Hobbs," she told him, "and having to postpone our wedding isn't going to change that. We'll get this business with Billy taken care of, then we can get married and do it right."

"But all the plans," Vincent protested. "The caterer, the band..."

Bari leaned forward and kissed Hobbs to quiet him, then said, "That won't be a problem. I've got my manager putting out feelers and I'm sure he's going to be able to find some high-rolling couple in town looking to get married in style. So we lose a little money on the napkins and matches. Who cares, huh?''

Vincent stared into the woman's eyes and exhaled through a tired smile. "You're wonderful," he told her.

"Takes one to know one," she replied. "Now let's go eat. I'm starved."

As they started for the door, Vincent reminded her, "Don't forget I want to take you by the trailer to meet my buddies afterward."

"I'm looking forward to it," she said, laughing, "as long as I don't have to jump out of a cake for them."

"Very funny, Bari."

"Just teasing."

Leaving the dressing room, the couple started down a long hallway leading to the escalators. On the way they passed a bank of telephone booths.

INSIDE THE BOOTH Ralph Calno dialed Wesley Burlington's home phone number.

"Yes?" Burlington answered.

"I bugged the room and heard 'em loud and clear," Calno reported. "He hasn't heard from the kid yet."

"I was hoping he had."

"Join the club."

"Well, we'll just have to keep trying, that's all."

"Did solve one other mystery, though."

"What's that?"

"You were right about Able Team. They moved into Hobbs's place when they checked out of the Dromedary."

"Good work, Ralph. That might come in handy down the line."

UNBEKNOWNST TO VINCENT, Billy Hobbs *had* called after being wounded by Ned Farrow. His message was on the answering machine when Able Team returned to the trailer after grabbing a bite to eat just down the block.

"I...I been shot, Uncle Vince," the message began. Hobbs's voice was high-pitched, strained with an edge of hysteria. "Bleeding a lot, but I'll...I'll be okay. The guy that shot me...name is Fairrrrrr..."

Lyons leaned over and turned up the volume, but all the three men were able to hear was the sound of traffic, then the voice of an operator requesting more money for another three minutes.

"Damn!" Lyons muttered, looking up from the machine. "You think he passed out?" he asked his partners.

Gadgets shook his head. "It sounded like he dropped the receiver and rushed off. Play it back again and check."

Lyons rewound the tape and they leaned closer as the message was repeated. "Yeah, I think I hear it, too," Lyons conceded. "Maybe he saw a cop."

"Or the man who shot him," Schwarz suggested.

"Yeah," Lyons said. He glanced over at Blancanales, who had just hung up the telephone and was now holding an ice pack where he'd bruised his elbow ducking the runaway car earlier that afternoon. "We've really got Lady Luck on our side this time, don't we?"

"*Sí,*" Blancanales groaned sarcastically. Eyeing the phone he said, "Struck out on this end, too. The cops ran a plate check on that Chevy. Stolen, just like I thought."

"But you saw skinheads inside, right?" Schwarz said.

Blancanales nodded, turning the ice pack over. He shivered slightly as he reapplied it to his elbow. "So either ARC knows we're here looking for them or else they're doing some more dirty work for Bobby Sumur's people." He went on to briefly explain Donna Alvarez's role in the mobster's imprisonment and why she was a likely target for their wrath.

"I hope she's taking a little more precaution now," Schwarz said. "As long as she's a viable witness, they're going to keep after her."

"I know, and I tried to tell her that," Blancanales said, "but she says she doesn't want to let fear run her life. She's determined to go about her normal business. I think I'll keep an eye on her, though, just the same."

"Gee, what a guy," Schwarz said, grinning. "And I bet it'll be a real chore for you, too, right?"

"Hah hah hah," Blancanales deadpanned, then looked over at Lyons. "What's our course now?"

Lyons got up and went to the window, peering through the shades at the trailer next door. "Well, Mrs. Yanders isn't back yet, so we can't get cracking on that meter man angle. I say we stick to the life-and-death matters at this point. We need to get to this Ned Farrow guy and tell him to back off Billy, and we should get some more protection for Donna, whether she likes it or not."

Blancanales went to the phone. "She gave me the name of her lawyer. I'll give him a call and have him lean on the Feds for a little witness protection. I think some of the Bureau people are due back today.''

"Good idea," Lyons said. "That would leave us free to cover all the bases on Farrow. I'll get his office address and stake out there.''

"I'll get his home," Schwarz volunteered.

"And I'll go to Global Imports and see if they can't call him off," Pol said as he waited for an answer on the phone.

As Blancanales started talking with Donna's lawyer, a car pulled up next to the trailer and Lyons peered out again, letting out a long, low whistle.

"Whoa, Vinnie baby," he muttered under his breath. "You lucky dog.''

Hobbs and Bari entered the trailer arm in arm, with Vincent showing obvious delight at the looks on the faces of his friends. He introduced his fiancée, bragging, "This lady sings and dances the way I cook.''

"Oh, don't listen to him," Bari scoffed modestly. "He's blinded by love.''

"Yeah, and what a way to go." Vincent laughed. His demeanor quickly changed, however, and he got down to more serious matters. "So, listen, guys. Any news about Billy on your end?''

"Yeah," Lyons said, "and it ain't good, I'm afraid.''

Hobbs's jaw slackened and he slumped into one of the kitchen chairs. Bari stood beside him, placing a comforting hand on his shoulder. "He's...is he okay?''

"He's been shot, Vinnie.''

"Oh, God. How bad?''

Lyons rewound the tape another time and played it back. Vincent's face whitened as he listened to his nephew's voice. He swallowed hard when the message ended. "Poor kid. He doesn't deserve this."

"Nobody does, Vinnie," Gadgets said. "Nobody does."

11

A pair of wide-rimmed sunglasses hid Ned Farrow's black eyes and most of the stitches he'd gotten at the hospital. The splint was still on his left hand, which he kept in his pocket as he hobbled into the Caravan, favoring the thigh he'd bruised when he'd fallen down the steps at the packing plant. He drew a few cursory stares as he worked his way through the crowd to an escalator reaching up to the second and third floors, where the Caravan's two showrooms were located. A tall man wearing a tuxedo stood before the escalator, checking for tickets from whoever wanted to get past him.

"Which show?" he asked Farrow.

"I'm not here for the damn show," Farrow muttered, flashing his identification. "Fries is expecting me."

The usher checked a small clipboard for Farrow's name, then stepped back to let the man pass. "Sorry, sir," he said in a voice totally devoid of apology.

"Don't sweat it, penguin."

Farrow rode up to the third floor, where patrons were already lining up for the ten-thirty show featuring sitcom star Mike Minner and the usual accompaniment of barely clad show girls. He walked past the crowd and around the corner to a back hallway. The guard recognized Farrow and let him pass. Halfway down the hall, the bounty hunter entered a room that served as an observation post overlooking the main casino. Security personnel were monitoring the action on banks of video monitors along one wall, and another wall was covered with one-way mirrors that allowed those inside the room to view the casino without being seen. Rick Fries was smoking a cigarette before the mirrors, staring down at the horde of gamblers while he spoke with Janice Kennesey. They stopped their conversation as Farrow came over to join them.

"Ned," Fries said. "I was surprised when I got your message. Burlington thought you'd be laid up at least until tomorrow."

"Can't keep a good man down," Farrow said with a grin, lowering his sunglasses just long enough to let Fries and Kennesey see the wounds he'd sustained from his clash with Billy Hobbs. "Besides, I'm not going to lay back and let somebody else take out the little shit that did this to me."

"Looks painful," Janice said.

"Only when I laugh," Farrow said.

"You shouldn't have much problem then," Fries quipped. "A sense of humor never was your strong suit."

Farrow slipped the sunglasses back up the bridge of his nose and took a step closer to Fries. "If I wanted to be a comedian, I'd audition for one of your shows, okay?"

"Hey, just kidding, for crying out loud," Fries muttered nervously. "Lighten up. What'd you want to see me about?"

"You know."

Fries exhaled and turned to the four security men in the room. "How about you guys get scarce for a few minutes?" The men obliged, leaving their equipment running so that Farrow, Fries and Kennesey continued to be bathed in the bluish glow of the monitors.

"What about her?" Farrow said, indicating the woman.

"I know what this is about," Janice said coolly, fitting a cigarette into her ivory holder. As Fries held a lighter in front of her and flicked a small flame to life, Kennesey stared past the first puff of smoke and focused her full concentration on Farrow. "I'm in."

"Since when?" Farrow demanded.

"Since I started laundering the skim around here through my warehouses," Kennesey responded evenly. "And don't act so surprised. You know that's what I was brought into the picture for."

"Yeah, I know that, but I didn't think you'd be sitting in with the big boys when we made our move," Farrow said.

"No reason a woman can't hold her own in this operation," Kennesey said. "But let's not waste valuable time on this, all right? All three of us have the same interest, and that's getting Vegas Bobby back here where he belongs and putting Burlington out to pasture. Right?"

Farrow didn't reply right away. He bought some time lighting a cigarette of his own. So Kennesey wanted in, huh? Interesting, he thought. He knew she and Fries had occasion to get into bed on more than business deals, and that alliance might throw off the tidy little balance of power Farrow had foreseen emerging once Vegas Bobby Sumur was back in command and Wes

Burlington and his back-east money were out of the picture. Farrow had envisioned the new organization having only three people calling the shots under Sumur—Fries, Clint Dirry and himself. They'd all worked together well in the past and could be trusted to respect one another's turf. But with Kennesey now being cut in for a slice of the action . . . that threw a little too much sway Fries's way. Farrow didn't like it. Not one bit.

But he wasn't about to let it show, at least not yet.

"Okay," Farrow said, "welcome to the club, Janice."

"Thank you, Ned." Her voice sounded no more sincere than his. She turned to Fries. "I take it this has something to do with greasing the skids for Bobby's new trial."

"Basically, yes," Fries said. "We've got to get this witness thing taken care of. The Simms boys botched their chance to get Alvarez this afternoon, and word is the Feds now have a three-man squad shadowing her round the clock, hoping to catch us making our next move.

"Calno's back east following Max Ernst around Atlantic City, and from the look of it there's only one private bodyguard to tend to on that front. Ralphie thinks he should be able to pop Ernst tonight."

"And what about Billy Hobbs?" Farrow asked. "Burlington told me he's got other people going after him besides me. That's fine, but I want to be the one who ices him, and I don't care what he says."

"Don't worry," Fries assured Farrow. "I've got my people out after him, and Alper's still got the cops on the case. If Billy gets spotted, they'll try to take him in so we can find out if he's spilled to anyone.''

"That's good enough for me," Farrow said. "And if I get to him first, you can be sure he'll talk, even if I have to yank his tongue out and wag it for him." Farrow glanced at Janice to see if she'd flinched at the imagery, but her face remained a clear, emotionless mask.

"As long as you're here," she told Farrow, "maybe I can get you to escort me across town with this."

She went over to a table, on the top of which was a black satchel filled with bundles of fifty- and hundred-dollar bills.

Farrow had made enough money runs in the past to know the bag contained at least a hundred thousand dollars, most of it undoubtedly collected under the table from various Caravan games and other "unofficial" activities generated by the syndicate. Kennesey would take the money and run it through her import accounting, then spit back a laundered share to the organization. For merely serving as a "guard" while the money was being transferred, Farrow knew he'd make a quick seven grand. He grinned at Janice. "Whatever you say, darlin'," he told her. "Whatever you say..."

MAX ERNST HAD BEEN NAMED after the famous German painter and sculptor, but the only art he'd ever taken an interest in was the art of deception. For the better part of twenty-five years Ernst, a longtime con artist and inveterate gambler, had come to Las Vegas twice a year on a personal holiday. Usually he would roll in with anywhere from three to thirty thousand dollars, most of it acquired through various shady business deals perpetrated within a six-state radius surrounding his native St. Louis. He would spend the bulk of it high-rolling his way from casino to casino, always with some buxom escort at his side and a muscle-bound flunky lurking nearby to make sure that no one tried to spoil his fun. He was always given a preferential welcome upon his arrival at any given establishment—ushered to a lavish suite and given complimentary champagne and room service—because he had a reputation for never being able to quit while ahead, and the house could be assured that they would receive a hefty return for their token perquisites. Vegas thrived on capricious big-stake losers like Ernst, whose cumulative losses more than made up for the slot jackpots paid off to the low-rent crowd.

Three years ago, however, Max Ernst had come to Vegas and checked into the Caravan with a different agenda in mind. He'd had a bad six months back in St. Louis, running afoul of creditors and falling under the scrutiny of federal investigators, and the nine grand he'd brought with him to Nevada—an amount swindled from a seventy-eight-year-old widow Ernst had charmed while visiting his mother in a nursing home—had constituted the whole of his wealth. His plan this time was to gamble the money until he'd at least tripled his holdings, then cash in and hustle his ass and the nest egg out of the country before the law could catch him. There were folks down in South America who could tide him over until the heat died down, then he figured he could return to the States and start fresh somewhere new, like San Diego.

Things hadn't worked out as planned, however.

From the outset, Ernst had been luckless no matter what game he tried. Blackjack, baccarat, craps, poker, the slots—he was cold on all fronts and his nine grand was lost the first night. Fortunately, his reputation was such that he was able to hit up Vegas Bobby Sumur, then shadow owner of the Caravan, for an extended line of credit. His losing streak had continued, and by the end of the week he was down by more than a hundred grand in markers. Despite his obvious inner panic, Ernst forged ahead with his usual bravado, assuring Sumur that he'd be good for the debt if he didn't manage to turn his luck around and at least break even.

After a particularly long night in one of the exclusive upper-floor poker rooms, however, Ernst had returned to his room to find he had visitors: Bobby Sumur, Ralph Calno and a human gorilla who made Ernst's bodyguard look like a chimpanzee. Ernst's bimbo and bodyguard had been asked to step outside so Ralph and Bobby could have "a little heart-to-heart with Maxie." Calno had just gotten back from St. Louis, where he'd been checking into Ernst's financial situation. Ralph and Bobby knew Ernst had no way to make good on his rising debt to the Caravan. The bottom line was simple: Ernst could do a few "favors" for Sumur, or else. To illustrate the "or else," Calno had shown Ernst a copy of that morning's paper, which detailed the shooting death of one Eric Alvarez in a back alley behind his nightclub. Ernst got the picture.

Vegas Bobby Sumur wanted Ernst to go back to St. Louis and help bait a trap whereby Sumur hoped to strike a decisive blow against the Cinzo crime family, longtime rivals of Sumur and his coterie of underworld friends. Sumur had reason to believe the Cinzos might try moving in on his Vegas turf and he wanted to discourage such a ploy. Ernst felt he had no choice but to comply with his "orders," but when he returned to Missouri another option presented itself. He was arrested by FBI agents on a handful of RICO counts and thrown into the slammer with prospects of doing more than a hundred years behind bars if convicted on all the charges against him.

Ernst had proposed a trade, his freedom for Vegas Bobby Sumur. His testimony, coupled with that of Donna Alvarez, had put Sumur and several underlings behind bars. As part of his deal, Ernst had been given plastic surgery, a new identity, a new home in New Jersey and limited protection in the form of a hired bodyguard. As Nat Stoops, Ernst had scaled down his earlier vices, although he still liked to indulge in gambling junkets to Atlantic City. With a reasonable amount of precaution, he'd been able to steer clear of the enemies he'd made by turning government witness.

Until tonight.

With Bobby Sumur jockeying for a new trial, his people had stepped up their efforts in recent months to track down Ernst, and the hard work had paid off. They'd finally made a contact within the Federal Witness Protection Program who'd uncovered Ernst's new identity.

Ralph Calno, in Atlantic City for less than two hours and battling the jet lag from his Vegas flight, stood at an island bar in the middle of the Boardwalk Casino, watching Ernst feed the pot at a nearby poker table. The Feds had done a good job in changing the man's appearance. With a shaved head, sculpted nose, bushy mustache and thirty-odd extra pounds clinging to his stocky frame, Ernst, as Nat Stoops, now looked nothing like the lean mop top who'd wined and dined his way through many a lost weekend in Vegas. Much of his earlier happy-go-lucky demeanor had changed as well. He played cards with grim concentration, all but ignoring the tall redheaded playmate seated beside him and the bodyguard busying himself with the keno slots a few yards away.

Calno himself had changed his appearance specifically for this assignment. Wearing a nondescript jogging outfit and a Redskins ball cap, the short man's face was covered with a convincing paste-on beard that matched the blondish/brown wig on his pointy head. He sat at the bar sipping a Tom Collins, throwing quarters down a countertop video poker game to bide his time as he waited for Ernst to finish playing.

Three-quarters of an hour later, Ernst got up from the table and ventured with the redhead to a cashier's booth, where he traded in his chips for currency. The bodyguard, a man of modest dimension but with the cold eyes of a predator, fell in with the twosome as they left the casino. Calno was a few dozen steps behind them. It was shortly after 4:00 a.m.

Outside, a harsh, cold wind was hurtling in from the Atlantic, and from the casino it was possible to see huge frothing whitecaps crashing against the shore less than fifty yards away. Most people were using other entrances and exits to the Boardwalk in hopes of avoiding the full brunt of the wind, so when Ernst and his two companions started across a long pedestrian walkway to the back parking structure, there was no one else about save for Calno.

Wearing soft-soled shoes, Calno was able to shorten the distance between himself and the others without drawing their attention. The howl of the wind and the crashing of the sea further masked his approach. When he was less than twelve yards away, however, the bodyguard glanced over his shoulder. A look of alarm came over his face and he reached into his coat, but it was too late.

Running at full force, Calno bent over as he charged into the bodyguard, clipping the man in the midsection with the impact of a defensive end looking to propel a linebacker out of bounds. The out-of-bounds line was the waist-high railing, and the bodyguard was knocked off balance, shouting with defiant surprise as he tumbled nearly fifty feet to the parking lot below, where he landed in a grotesque heap between a Porsche and Jaguar.

The redhead screamed and recoiled in horror as Calno turned on Ernst, who was trying to get out a handgun from his coat.

"No go, Maxie," Calno told the man as he pinned Ernst's arms behind his back and shoved him against the railing. Ernst tried to struggle, but he was outmatched by the shorter man's feverish intensity, and moments later he, too, fell to his death a few feet away from his would-be protector. Chest heaving from the exertion of his efforts, Calno turned to the woman, who was about to run off. He grabbed her by the arm and pulled her close, staring at her with malicious eyes. "Windy out, isn't it?" he told her as he dragged her to the railing, "So bad there's liable to be some freak accidents before things quiet down."

12

By morning, Ned Farrow had failed to show up at either his home or his office, so Pol Blancanales followed through on the plan Able Team had discussed the previous night and drove to the corporate headquarters of Global Imports. It was located in a newly erected office building on East Charleston, near an even newer subdivision within teeing distance of the Desert Rose Golf Course.

Global occupied the entire penthouse suite, and when Pol stepped out of the elevator he found himself in the reception area, a large room with a light pastel color scheme that reminded him of a "Miami Vice" rerun he'd seen back at the Dromedary the other night. Huge potted succulents flanked a long leather couch, and on one wall was a massive oil painting of the Global Imports logo as seen through the eyes of someone with an obvious fondness for Matisse. A young receptionist with teased hair and an accommodating smile looked up at Pol from her desk.

"Can I help you?"

Blancanales approached the desk, pulling out his cover identification card and handing it to the woman. "I need to speak to Ms Kennesey," he said, having been given the name by Aaron Kurtzman during a phone call earlier in the morning.

"I don't believe she's expecting you," the receptionist said.

Pol could see she was suitably impressed by his credentials, however, and he insisted, "If you could just check in with her. Tell her it concerns Ned Farrow and Billy Hobbs."

The woman silently mouthed the names to herself as she picked up a phone and dialed one of the extension numbers. Pol wandered away from the desk and gazed out a picture window facing eastward. He could see the gambling empire in the distance, stretching the length of Las Vegas Boulevard from McCarran International Airport on up to the downtown casinos around Fremont and South Main. Beyond that, a few remnants of snow still clung to Potosi Mountain, at 8500 feet the highest peak of the Spring Mountain range. At this time of year, Vegas looked its best, like the crisp, clear-aired fantasy oasis it was designed to be. A few months down the line, as temperatures crept up to the three-digit mark, the air would take on a less hospitable hue and the whole city would feel the wilting effects of the oppressive heat and the full influx of the summer tourist season. Pol had made the mistake once of coming to Vegas in July. And only once.

"Mr. Blancanales," the receptionist called out, rising from her desk. "Ms Kennesey can see you in her office. If you'll follow me..."

"Gladly," Pol said with a warm smile, forcing a reddish blush to creep up the woman's neck.

"Will you be wanting anything to drink?" she asked him.

"No thanks."

They went through a back archway to a hall lined with mahogany doors. One of them opened and Janice Kennesey stepped out to greet Pol.

"Mr. . . . Blancanales, was it?"

"Yes," Pol said, shaking the woman's hand and following her into her office as the receptionist returned to her desk.

Kennesey's suite carried on with the same scheme as the waiting room, down to the plants and another logo painting. Gesturing to one of the leather chairs near her desk, Janice said, "Have a seat."

She circled around and sat behind her desk, picking up a mug of still-steaming coffee. There were papers before her on the desk blotter, and she started going over them with a pen as she spoke.

"You'll excuse me, Mr. Blancanales, but these papers have to be expressed over to Boulder City by noon..."

"No problem."

"What was it you wished to discuss?" she asked without looking up from her chore.

"We understand you've contracted a bounty hunter to track down Billy Hobbs for allegedly robbing one of your warehouses the other night," Pol said. "His name is Ned Farrow."

"Yes, that's correct," Kennesey said matter-of-factly. "One of our longtime employees was killed during that robbery. We feel we owe it to him and to his family to make an additional effort to see that justice is served."

"With all due respect, Ms Kennesey," Pol said, "we have reason to believe the Hobbs youth might be innocent, and we'd like to see—"

"Innocent?" Kennesey scoffed, looking up from her papers. "If he's so innocent, why is he hiding out like a coward? And why did he attack Mr. Farrow when he tried to bring him in yesterday afternoon?"

"What was that again?" Pol was stunned. There'd been no mention of any encounter between Farrow and Hobbs when Able Team had contacted the police both the previous night and earlier this morning.

Kennesey signed the last document and started stuffing the papers into an express mailer. "Mr. Farrow was trying to bring Mr. Hobbs into custody when that youngster attacked him. Nearly blinded him and sent him to the hospital for stitches, mind you. Hardly the actions of an innocent man."

"So that's where Farrow must have been last night," Pol thought aloud.

Kennesey eyed him blankly, showing no sign that she had a much more accurate idea as to where Farrow had been. The two of them had wound up at her condominium on the south side, making out with abandon on her king-size bed, then lying side by side between silk sheets as they'd discussed the impending realignment of their little power clique in Vegas if and when Vegas Bobby Sumur was let out of prison and Wes Burlington was bumped out of the picture. She liked the way things were shaping up thus far. Both Farrow and Rick Fries enjoyed sex with her, and she was sure that she could play the two against each other to better her own standing in the organization.

She listened attentively as Pol laid out all he knew about the mysterious circumstances surrounding the theft of the handgun used in the warehouse robbery, about Billy Hobbs's prison stint and the youth's determination to avoid being put behind bars at any cost, concluding, "And I think you'll have to agree with me that no justice will be served if Ned Farrow kills Billy and it turns out that somebody else was responsible for shooting your guard."

Kennesey glanced down at the notes she'd taken while Pol had been talking, taking great care to show no overt response aside from a look of impartiality. When she looked back up at Blancanales, she nodded slowly and said, "The way you explain it, I have to confess you have a point."

"Thank you."

"So, as I understand it, you're asking me to take Ned Farrow off assignment and let you handle things."

"In a word, yes," Pol said.

"And I suppose that if I refuse, you have the authority to order me to do it anyway."

Pol smiled slightly and offered a so-so wave of the hand. "It's a gray area, but we'd be forced to at least try. There is a life at stake here, after all."

"Well, Mr. Blancanales, it won't be necessary," the woman said, rising from her chair. "I can see this from your perspective and I'm willing to play along... provided that your people would be willing to compensate Global Imports for any fees that might be owed to Mr. Farrow, of course."

"Of course," Pol said, extending his hand for another shake. "Thank you so much, Ms Kennesey."

"I'll walk you out," she said, picking up the express envelope. On the way out of her office, she said, "If it's any help, I spoke to Farrow less than an hour ago, and he was acting on a tip that Billy was seen wandering outside of town near Boulder Highway. Could be Hobbs was going to try to hitch a ride to Boulder City."

"I'll check it out," Pol said, holding the door open for Kennesey. "Where exactly was he spotted?"

"On Russell Road, near Duck Creek," Janice lied. "If you have a map it's easy to find."

"Great," Pol said. "I'll get right on it."

The two of them walked as far as the archway, then parted company. Kennesey walked nonchalantly back into her office, but as soon as she had closed the door behind her, she rushed to her desk and dialed the number of Ned Farrow's car phone.

"Hello?" the bounty hunter answered.

"Ned, it's Janice."

"Hey, babe, I was missing you, too. Some night, I gotta—"

"Ned," Janice interrupted. "Listen carefully."

BILLY HOBBS WAS nowhere near Duck Creek.

He was more than ten miles away, cramped into a human ball in the back of a half-crushed Ford Econoline van discarded in one of the back rows of the salvage yard where he'd sought refuge the night the whole sorry ordeal had begun.

Billy grimaced as a sensation of all-consuming pain, which had overcome him a few short hours ago, now served an opposite effect, rousing him from his troubled, nightmare-plagued sleep. Fever blazed across his forehead, mingling sweat with his blood, yet despite his temperature he shivered as a breeze crept through the van's broken windows and blew against his drenched clothing.

He could barely recall dragging his battered body back to this refuge the previous night. The only vivid images in his mind were those of the struggle with Ned Farrow back at the packing plant, mixed with some dim recollection of charging through a sea of brittle mesquite, feeling the sting of branches slapping against his already tortured flesh.

The pain he felt now was so pervasive that he wept out of sheer agony and misery for the better part of twenty minutes, purging himself as best he could. When the jag passed, he lay still a while longer, then shifted his body and shoved one leg against the side door of the van. It swung open, letting in the brilliant, almost torturous morning light.

"G...g...got to m...move," he croaked hoarsely, feeling dried blood crackle along his parched lips.

In addition to his pain, Billy was stiff from the position he'd slept in, and when he finally managed to pry himself out of the van, he walked with a slow, tentative gait. Several times he was forced to slump against the side of some twisted chassis and pause, riding out a feeling of faintness that seemed ever on the verge of drawing a dark curtain across his mind.

"H...help," he whispered to the unhearing mounds of four-wheelers around him.

It took him more than a half hour of stopping and starting to travel a mere forty yards, but that distance was sufficient to place him at the edge of the salvage yard, near the tall cyclone fence he'd scaled the first time he'd trespassed onto the property. He'd been much stronger then, and this time when he came up against the barrier, Billy's jaw dropped slowly and he let out a long, low moan as he dropped slowly to his knees.

"P... please," he sobbed.

His cry was answered by a deep, guttural growling behind him. Turning slightly, Billy glanced back and saw a hundred-pound Rottweiler staring at him, yellow-fanged jaws exposed below its glistening eyes. The dog stayed in place, and presently a middle-aged man in greasy coveralls and carrying a double-barreled shotgun stepped into view. He took one look at Billy Hobbs and shook his head.

"Easy, boy," he told his dog. "Looks like this poor bastard's already been chewed up, but good..."

LEAVING THE CITY BEHIND, Blancanales continued driving south toward Russell Road, keeping his eyes open for any trace of either Ned Farrow or Billy Hobbs. As he rolled to a stop at a forlorn intersection, he glanced at his rearview mirror and noticed metallic glints in the sky behind him. Shifting into idle, Pol rolled down his window and leaned his head out so he could get a better look.

Roughly ten miles to the north was Nellis Air Force Base, and Pol quickly realized that the glints were caused by sunlight glancing off the sides of gleaming fighter jets being piloted above the desert flats by members of the Thunderbirds. Even from this far away he could see the jets weave through their intricate maneuvers and he felt a twinge of jealousy. He had no doubt that being at the controls of a speeding T-bird as it thundered through the sky had a special rush all its own, perhaps matching the sensation he and his compatriots in Able Team felt when they were in the thick of combat with their lives on the line. Jack Grimaldi, crackerjack pilot on many missions for the men from Stony Man Farm, had often described the feeling, and the few times Pol had shared the cockpit in some winged wonder like an F-16, he'd had a sense of that exhilaration.

"Okay, Chevy, do your stuff," he murmured sarcastically as he shifted his rental car back into gear and drove off, turning his attention back to matters closer at hand.

Just as he was reaching for his palm-sized communicator so that he could put a call through to Schwarz and Lyons about his meeting with Kennesey, Blancanales was distracted by yet another out-of-the-ordinary action falling into range of his peripheral vision. This time, however, the source of the distraction was much closer. A pale gray Dodge station wagon had materialized from out of a ditch flanking the road and was speeding directly toward him in a cloud of dust raised by its madly spinning wheels.

"What the hell!"

Pol dropped the communicator and grabbed the steering wheel with both hands as he stomped on the brakes and tried to avoid colliding with the Dodge. Rubber bit at the asphalt and the Chevy skidded sideways, coming to an abrupt and jarring halt as it slammed into the station wagon.

The impact flung Pol forward and it was only the restraining force of his shoulder belt that kept him from being impaled against the steering wheel and possibly thrown through the windshield. As it was, the suddenness of the stop forced the wind from his lungs and he drew blood as his forehead struck the rearview mirror. Stunned by the blow, Pol nonetheless acted on well-honed instincts and reached inside his coat for his .45.

Both front doors of the Dodge swung open and the Simms twins burst out, each of them brandishing a small .22 automatic. They charged the Chevy, drawing bead on Pol as Ned Farrow pulled up from behind in his white Mustang.

"Go ahead, asshole," B.L. Simms taunted Blancanales, coming up next to the driver's side of the Nova and pressing his weapon against Pol's bleeding forehead. "Pull that gun out. Force me to drill one right between your fucking eyes!"

"That's good enough, B.L.," Ned called out as he emerged from the convertible and ambled over. "Let's hold off on the lobotomy for right now, okay?"

Simms reluctantly pulled the gun away from Pol's head. That same instant, Blancanales suddenly lunged into motion, opening his door with all his strength and bowling B.L. off his feet. In the same movement, he pulled out his Colt and was prepared to use it to take out as many of the enemy as he could, when Kenny Simms bounded over the hood of the Chevy and tackled him. Pol's shot went into the dirt and he grunted as Kenny took him down. The other twin quickly recovered and joined in the fracas.

Though Blancanales fared well considering the odds, he was too dazed from the collision to pose a serious threat, and Farrow put an end to his fight by clipping Pol behind the ear with the butt of his Casull .454. The ground came up to greet Blancanales, and the world for him went black.

"One down," Farrow told the twins as he holstered his Casull. "Two to go..."

13

Ned Farrow's office was located above a minimart complex at the corner of Horseshoe Lane and Sagebrush Drive, less than a five-minute drive from his home. None of the stores were open yet and Carl Lyons felt conspicuous as he sat behind the wheel of his Nova, one of the three Chevys rented by Able Team since their arrival in Vegas. Parked across the street from the complex since late last night, Lyons had nursed a thermos of coffee and two deli sandwiches during his vigil, most of which had been spent huddled low in the front seat so as to avoid detection by those few motorists traveling through this newly developed section of town just outside the city limits. Under cover of night, he'd felt far less visible, but now he was forced to maintain his surveillance in the daylight.

He'd bought three different morning papers shortly after they were delivered to the stands down the block, and he read with interest a short article about the incident in front of Pedro's Mexican diner the previous afternoon. Donna Alvarez was mentioned by name, but Pol was referred to only as "a federal agent" speaking with her about possible testimony in the new trial being sought by Vegas Bobby Sumur. No official connection was made between the incident and rumored threats against Donna, but the message was clearly conveyed between the lines.

Setting aside the paper, Lyons reached for his communicator, adjusting the broadcasting mode so he could link up with the FBI agents assigned to watch over Donna Alvarez. The officer in charge of the detail informed Lyons that there had been no trouble during the night and that the woman was presently back at the Mission, supervising the breakfast food lines. Lyons placed another call to Sergeant Alper at the police station and was told that Billy Hobbs was still at large.

"No news is good news," he whispered to himself as he set the communicator aside, only half believing his words. There was something about the way this whole Vegas mess was unfolding that bothered Lyons, and as he mulled it over he realized it was a disturbing sense of déjà vu, harking back to the late seventies, when, after six years with the LAPD he'd been taken off his regular beat and put on the Department's Organized Crime Unit. None of his previous police training had truly prepared him for kind of pervasive evils attributed to his newly targeted enemy. Mafia, LCN, Cosa Nostra, the syndicate—there were subtle differences between each designation, but it was a matter of semantics as far as Lyons had been concerned, because on the whole organized crime operated under one unifying code—feed the greed at any cost.

When his reckless but effective approach to his job drew the eventual attention of the Feds and led to his recruitment into the Justice Department's Organized Crime Strike Force, Lyons had a chance to butt heads with crime families from one end of the coast to the other, and the more mobsters he dealt with, the more he realized they were all stamped from the same ruthless, self-serving mold.

After being recruited to Stony Man Farm's Able Team, Lyons had been able to move on to a wider smorgasbord of human scum, tackling drug peddlers, international terrorists, serial killers and other assorted vermin, but still it was rare when a year would pass without his once again crossing paths with his old nemeses.

And now he was mired in the thick of one of organized crimes most widely renowned breeding grounds. Although the Mob element had waned considerably since the days when Bugsy Siegel operated out of the original Flamingo, Lyons didn't buy the noise that the city was now clean of criminal influence. It just didn't wash. There was too much easy money to be made in this town, and organized crime liked nothing better than easy money. No, Lyons was certain that the Mob was thick as thieves behind the woodwork of Vegas, perhaps not dipping their hands into the tills of every casino, but nonetheless exerting their will sufficiently enough to carve out an empire defended by hired shills and goons like the skinhead punks from the Aryan Right Coalition.

Lyons could feel his anger rising the more he dwelt on the situation, and meshing with his fatigue and hunger, the loathing became so strong he felt his muscles knotting with the cumulative tension. Getting out of his car, he stretched his limbs and looked upward, letting the sun warm his face.

A convenience store down the block was just opening up. Lyons decided to wander down and grab some more provisions. As he was moving around his car to the sidewalk, he heard a car pull out of an alley behind him. Instinctively on his guard, he glanced over his shoulder, just in time to see an Ingram submachine gun poke out of the back window of a screeching Hyundai.

"Shit!" Lyons flattened himself against the sidewalk as .45 ACP slugs ripped across the top of his Chevy and shattered windows in the storefront of a real estate office behind him. He crawled closer to his car, using it for cover as the Hyundai whizzed past, then started making a U-turn in the intersection.

Yanking open the passenger's door, Lyons scrambled across the front seat and got behind the wheel, cranking his engine to life as he pulled out his Government Model and fired at his would-be assassins. He didn't take out the other driver, but he bought enough time to get his own car going. Making a sharp right at the first driveway he came to, Lyons sped between buildings to the back alley. To his amazement, a second enemy vehicle, this one a Ford pickup, nearly broadsided him as he raced for the nearest side street. A skinhead passenger in the truck fired at Lyons with a .357 Magnum, shattering the Chevy's windshield.

Lyons swerved his car, bowling over a row of trash cans as he whisked clear of the pickup. Flooring the accelerator, Ironman put some distance between both the Ford and the Hyundai, which had sped back into the chase from the same alley Lyons had fled down.

Driving with one hand, Lyons used the other to grab his communicator and key it so he could get a message through to Schwarz.

"Mayday, Gadgets!" he exclaimed. "Ambush!"

LYONS'S WARNING was old news to Schwarz.

After eleven hours of uneventful stakeout down the road from Farrow's isolated Mesquite Haven home, Gadgets's Nova had been abruptly bombarded by Ingram blasts that left him unscathed but rendered the car inoperable. Rather than remain a sitting duck for his unseen assassins, Schwarz rolled from the vehicle and lived through a .45 ACP death dance as he ran for the cover of huge concrete sewer line segments laid out parallel to the road.

He was catching his breath to the accompaniment of gunfire and ricocheting slugs off cement when Lyons's message bleeped over the communicator clipped to his waist.

"Thanks for the warning," Gadgets muttered glibly. "I'd hang on and talk but I have company."

Setting his M-1911 on semiautomatic, Schwarz shifted position as the enemy fire skimmed off the sewer pipe only a few inches from his head, stinging his cheek with shrapnel. He dived through the inside of the pipe, did an acrobatic somersault, then spun around as he came back to his feet, intuitively tracing the trajectory of the last shot and lining up his target over the automatic's phosphorus sights.

A young man in combat fatigues was straddling a pipe twenty yards away, readying to unleash another round of fire. Schwarz triggered his .45 first, and thanks to the increased twist of the Colt's barrel rifling, the accuracy of his shot was deadly. The sniper on the pipes took the shots in the face and upper torso, all but one of them enough on the mark to have killed him. The Ingram tumbled to the soft earth while the ambusher lay dead where he was hit, blood coursing down the bleached gray curvature of the pipe.

Gadgets had little time to celebrate, because there were three other ARC goons out to get him, and one of them was behind the wheel of a Ford Ranger that roared onto the scene, scraping its passenger side as it cornered too sharply around one of the cement pipes and bore down on Schwarz. Gadgets was off balance, having leaned over in hopes of grabbing the stray Ingram, and it was all he could do to lunge between pipes at the last second to avoid being flattened by the truck.

Schwarz had gone up against three-to-one odds many a time, both in the jungles of Vietnam and other supposedly more civilized hellholes across the globe, and one of the main reasons he'd survived such encounters was that he knew when it was best to stage a strategic retreat and try to shift the battle to suit his terms.

Drawing in a deep breath, Schwarz drew a mental image of the layout around him, then bolted out between the pipes, making a diving somersault back to his car. As anticipated, he drew fire from the two gunmen on the ground, and once he placed their positions, he used the rest of his fifteen-round magazine pinning them back to buy himself a few extra seconds. The man in the truck was halfway down the block, looking for a break in the pipeline so he could cut back onto the road. It was now or never.

"Now!" Schwarz screamed to himself as he made his move.

Breaking away from his car, Schwarz zigzagged across a level plot of land where the foundation for a new home had been laid, and stacks of lumber provided him with some cover as he headed for the wash bordering the development. A cross fire between his two pedestrian pursuers nearly brought him down several times, but he was adept enough in his evasive maneuvers to reach the arroyo unharmed. Dropping over the side, he lowered himself out of the view of those coming after him. He knew from experience that they would immediately slow down, not knowing which way he might flee down the wash and where he might show up. As it turned out, once he was halfway down the steep slope of the ditch, Schwarz stayed put. True, he was still the prey, but now he could play this lethal game of cat and mouse with a mind toward offense as well as defense. Reaching into his pocket, he removed a fresh ammo magazine and fed it into the Colt. Fifteen shots, three targets. The odds were looking better all the time. It was just a matter of perspective.

Remote as the corner of the development was, there were few competing sounds for Schwarz to have to sort through, and he was able to hear the approach of his attackers without having to betray his position. One at a time, he thought to himself, blocking out his strategy. Schwarz-in-a-box. When he detected that one of the men was nearing the wash off to his left, he popped up into view. The gunman wasn't expecting him to be in the same place he'd fallen from view, and by the time he turned to face Schwarz, the skinhead had four holes in his chest. He curled from the impact of the slugs, slumping face first into the dirt.

As he dropped back into the wash, Schwarz caught both the truck and the second gunman out of the corner of his eye, and, in the same action, he deliberately dived in one direction, then promptly doubled back and ran the opposite way, to huddle finally, behind a fifty-gallon metal drum half-buried in the sand.

Five seconds later, he saw the second gunman crawling on his belly to the lip of the wash and looking in the direction he thought Schwarz had taken. At the same time, the Ford Ranger rolled over the side and down the steep slope, with the driver wrestling for control with one hand on the wheel and the other holding a Beretta automatic.

Gadgets drew bead on the closest man and waited until he was looking his way before pulling the trigger. Five nonstop blasts of the Government Model slammed into the assailant, knocking him from his belly onto his back so that his mouth hung open and his lifeless eyes stared up at the morning sun.

The man in the pickup saw what had happened to his two partners and decided against trying to finish off his assignment alone. He used the Ranger's four-wheel drive for added traction, churning up fantails of sand as he tried to make his getaway.

Bounding to his feet, Schwarz charged after the truck, holding one arm before him to shield his eyes from the spray of sand. He spent the rest of his ammo trying to disable the Ford and its driver, but it was like taking target practice in a blizzard, and although he rattled the bodywork and took out yet another window, he couldn't prevent the truck from muscling its way back up onto solid ground and speeding off down the service road.

"Damn," he murmured, giving up the chase.

Walking back to the slain youth at the edge of the wash, Schwarz shook his head in disgust. The assailant couldn't have been more than twenty years old and had something of a baby face. He had swastikas tattooed on his knuckles and in one ear he wore the decorative skull and crossbones of Hitler's SS.

"What a waste." Schwarz spit in the dirt. When would the world ever learn? he wondered bitterly as he headed back toward his Nova. Before he reached it, he saw a cloud of dust announcing the arrival of another vehicle. Schwarz reached inside the Chevy for another clip of ammunition but didn't bother loading it into his .45 when he recognized the car as a twin to his own Nova.

Lyons pulled up next to Schwarz and quickly surveyed the battle zone.

"One of them got away," Schwarz told him.

"The guys chasing me gave up halfway here," Lyons said. "Someone must have tipped them off."

"Seems that way," Schwarz agreed. "At least we got through it."

"I'm not so sure about that," Lyons said, glancing up at Schwarz from behind the wheel. "I can't get anything from Pol."

14

Vincent Hobbs had spent the night at Bari's apartment, calling his trailer periodically in hopes of hearing some good news regarding his nephew on the answering machine. The only messages he had received, however, were from work. One was from his boss at the city desk, who wanted Vincent to dig deeper into the story of Donna Alvarez and her work with the homeless, tying in recent actions by the Aryan Right Coalition and the alleged link between the white supremacists and any local syndicate activity. The other was from a periodic writing partner who was volunteering to run with any loose ends on the story and even take it over if Vincent and Bari wanted to take some time off for a honeymoon after their wedding.

Wedding.

Vincent felt miserable about the way Billy's troubles had fouled up his plans to marry Bari, but at the same time her understanding and support assured him all the more that he was making the right decision in asking her to be his wife. On his way back to the trailer that morning, he stopped off at a florist's and made arrangements to have a bouquet of roses sent to Bari's dressing room that night along with the message: "It'll be worth waiting for, I promise."

There was no sign that Able Team had returned to the trailer when Vincent let himself in to take a shower and change his clothes. He wasn't overly concerned, however, because he recalled from his days at the Farm that when the men went out on assignment, they had a tendency to lose all track of time, operating by the guiding principle that the enemy didn't work by the clock, either. In particular he remembered one mission during which the Team had been forced to do without sleep or food for eighty-one hours straight when they had tracked down a band of kidnappers who'd taken an oil heiress hostage in the barren wilds of the Mojave Desert.

When he got out of the shower, Hobbs put through a call to the police station and asked to speak to Sergeant Alper. The officer reported no new developments in the search for Hobbs's nephew, and no, he hadn't heard from Able Team since late the previous night.

"One other thing," Vincent said, "I'm doing a story on Donna Alvarez and this whole business with Bobby Sumur and ARC. Any chance I could drop by sometime today and pick your brains on it?"

There was a pause at the end of the line, then Alper told him, "I'm not really on top of that one, Vince. We got a separate team handling things there. If you want, I can put in a word for you and have someone get back to you. You at home or the office?"

"I'll be home for another half hour," Vincent said, checking the clock, "then I'm off to work."

"Okay, I'll see what I can do."

"Thanks, Sarge."

"No problem."

Vince hung up and went through his refrigerator, coming up with some eggs and enough trimmings to put together an omelet while he watched the morning news. Halfway through a dry filler piece about tourism in the city, the TV anchorman was handed a bulletin and interrupted the story to report news of a shoot-out at the Mesquite Haven housing development in which there were at least two confirmed fatalities, both of them alleged members of the Aryan Right Coalition. Vince noted the details, concluding from the outset that somehow Able Team was involved, even though they weren't shown on screen and the on-site reporter referred to them only as members of a special federal task force.

Moments after the segment finished, the phone rang. Vincent was certain it would be either someone from the Team or the man Alper had referred him to. He was wrong on both counts.

It was someone from the University Medical Center.

"Are you related to a William Hobbs?" the emotionless voice asked.

"Yes, I'm his uncle," Vincent said, feeling a cold chill run down his spine.

"Are you his legal guardian?"

"Yes, damn it! What's wrong?"

"Well, sir, your nephew was brought in here a few minutes ago with a bullet wound and other injuries. He's lost a lot of blood and they'll be taking him for trauma surgery shortly. We just wanted to find out if he has any insurance and what—"

"I'll cover his bills! Just take care of him!" Vincent said.

"Fine, sir. Now, if you could just give me the name of your carrier, I'll go ahead and—"

"I'm on my way!" he snapped. "We can handle that shit later."

Slamming down the phone, Vincent turned off the range and left his omelet half-cooked in the frying pan. Rushing into the bedroom, he quickly threw on some clothes and bounded to the front door, car keys in hand.

"Well, well, Mr. Hobbs," Ned Farrow said, blocking the doorway. "You must be psychic. I was just about to ring the bell."

"Who are you?" Vince said irritably. "I'm in a hurry."

"Oh, that's good," Ned said, reaching inside his coat and withdrawing his Casull .454. "So am I."

15

"He left here at least a couple of hours ago," Janice Kennesey told Carl Lyons and Gadgets Schwarz, responding calmly to their queries regarding the whereabouts of Pol Blancanales. They were standing in the reception area at Global Imports headquarters.

"Did he mention where he was going?" Schwarz asked.

"Let me think." Kennesey paused a moment, staring absently out the picture window as if trying to collect her thoughts. "I believe he mentioned something about meeting up with two friends."

"Well, he never made it that far," Lyons said, "and we haven't been able to reach him."

"I'm sorry," Kennesey said. "I wish I could be of more help, but that's really all I know."

"Have you been in touch with Ned Farrow since you talked to Blancanales?" Schwarz asked her.

The woman shook her head as she fit a cigarette into her ivory holder with slow, precise movements, making sure the men saw no sign of nervous twitching. She lit the cigarette and blew smoke as she shook her head. "He wasn't at his office or at home," she said. "However, I did leave messages at both places that he was to stop looking for Billy Hobbs."

"Do you think he'll follow your orders?" Lyons asked.

"I don't see why he shouldn't," Kennesey lied. "This was strictly a business arrangement for Ned. I said that your people would be paying for his time, plus the bonus he would have received for bringing Hobbs in, so there's really no reason for him to stay on the case, is there?"

"I don't know," Lyons said. "Is there?"

"I'm not sure what you're getting at."

"Well, Ms Kennesey, we've heard Farrow tends to take his job too seriously, that he's worse than the Royal Canadian Mounties about making sure he always gets his man. It might be that he'll still go after Billy just as a matter of pride."

"I seriously doubt that," the woman insisted, "but I don't have any control over his actions. Look, gentlemen, I think I've been more than reasonable and cooperative about all of this, and I do still have a business to run, so if you will excuse me . . ."

Lyons and Schwarz traded glances. It was clear that they were spinning their wheels here. Gadgets turned to Janice and handed her a business card with Vince Hobbs's number on the back. "This is our number while we're in town. If you remember anything else, please call us, okay?"

"I'll do that." Kennesey led them to the elevators. "And when Mr. Blancanales checks in with you, I'm sure he'll vouch for everything I've told you."

The elevator doors opened and the two men stepped in. As the doors hissed closed and they headed down to the ground floor, Lyons turned to Schwarz. "You think she's on the level?"

"I want to think so," Schwarz said, "but my gut says otherwise."

"Good. That makes two of us. I wish we had some more coverage so we could throw a shadow on this place, but I don't want to pull any of the Feds off Donna at this point."

"And you don't trust the cops?" Schwarz said.

"It's not so much that I don't trust them," Lyons said. "I just don't think this whole business is too high on their list of priorities. I get the feeling that Alper's only plugging his dimmest bulbs into the task force. I'd rather do without that kind of help."

"I guess so." The elevator reached the ground floor and the men headed out of the lobby to the parking lot. Schwarz went through his pockets for keys to the Nova. "All the same, though, if Pol doesn't check in soon, I say we come back here with a fine-tooth comb."

"Fair enough." As he got into the passenger's side of the Nova, Lyons sighed. "What the hell, let's swing by the station and rattle their cages again. Who knows, maybe we'll be lucky and find some decent help."

ANYONE WHO THINKS all airports look alike has never been to McCarran International in Las Vegas. Granted, the architecture and internal decor may be interchangeable with any number of terminals around the world. But Vegas is one of the few places on earth where slot machines are lined up like sentries just outside the boarding gates, ready to clean the pockets of any poor souls anxious to either start or end their gambling fix within earshot of the jumbo jets that brought them to this strange mecca of glitter and greed.

Looking to kill a little time, Wesley Burlington peeled a hundred-dollar bill from his money clip and cashed it in for coins so he could play the dollar slots near Gate 8B. Whenever he played the slots, Burlington used the same strategy—progressive video poker, five coins at a time, save half the winnings and keep on playing with the rest. Provided he hit a couple of winners early to cover the initial investment, he could always count on at least doubling his take. A few times he'd hung on long enough to pull the royal flush payoff, usually more than a thousandfold return.

Not that he needed to bother himself with such trite diversions as a means of making money—after all, in the time it would take him to play one round on a machine, his stockbroker could be making him a few hundred thousand dollars with a single well-placed call. But Burlington nursed this quirk more as a means of keeping himself in touch with the average tourists in town, the middle-class folks who pumped the bulk of the money into Las Vegas. Burlington felt that he could successfully exploit those people by staying on top of the desires that motivated them. This was a vital point, as there was a certain magic that had to be fostered and maintained in order to lure people back time and again when the town's odds were against them and when they'd left losers.

Playing methodically as he did, Burlington went through his hundred dollars and his divided winnings in ten minutes flat. He cashed in what was left and found out that he'd lost fifty-eight dollars total. He pocketed the forty-two and wandered closer to the gate, where a flight attendant announced that the American

West flight from St. Louis had just landed and its passengers would be disembarking in a moment.

Glancing to his right, Burlington saw that Sergeant Alper was still in one of the phone booths. He was wearing a tan suit that no doubt fit him better thirty pounds ago. Alper had half turned his back to the door to better guard his privacy, but Burlington could still see enough of the man's face to tell he was upset.

Not another screw up, I hope, Burlington thought to himself. There had been too many of those already. It was a disturbing trend that needed serious tending to. The kind of grand schemes he had in mind for Vegas needed to be built on a solid foundation, a foundation of competent underlings. A good organization. Why else would they call it "organized" crime?

Passengers began to enter the lounge, spilling down a tunneled walkway into the terminal. Burlington searched their faces. There were many businessmen in suits, usually a sign that several conventions were in town. Ralph Calno was among the last to emerge from the plane. He was carrying his suit jacket draped over one arm and was holding a carryon bag in the other. When he caught Burlington's gaze, he nodded perfunctorily and broke away from the other passengers to join him. The men shook hands and strode over to the cocktail lounge across from the booth where Alper was wrapping up his phone call. It wasn't until a waiter had taken their orders and gone off for a pitcher of martinis that Calno spoke.

"You heard, I take it."

Burlington nodded. "It was on the news this morning. Terrible gust of wind."

"Very," Calno said. "Poor fools should have known better than to go walking out there when it was so bad."

"I knew we could count on you."

"I'm glad." Calno crossed his hands on the table. "And how are things faring here?"

"Not as well, I'm afraid," Burlington said. "The Alvarez woman has Fed protection around the clock now, and the Hobbs boy's still out there somewhere. On top of all that, a couple of ARC boys got themselves killed trying to ambush Able Team."

Calno shook his head in disgust. "I was never too keen on bringing the skinheads in. They're nothing but amateurs, if you ask me."

The waiter returned with their pitcher and three glasses. Burlington paid from his money clip and poured drinks as Alper finally joined them.

"Schwarz and Lyons just stopped by the station," Alper told Burlington after acknowledging Calno with a curt nod.

"Byrne deal with them?" Burlington asked.

"Yeah. Fed 'em the whole hook, line and sinker. He thinks they bought it."

"What are you talking about?" Calno asked.

Alper explained, "Lieutenant Byrne's with our organized crime unit. Our fox guarding the henhouse. He dummied up a report on that burglary at Vincent Hobbs's trailer and put together a fake composite of somebody who doesn't look anything like you, so they're gonna be off the scent."

"I don't follow," Calno said.

"You need me to paint you a picture?" Alper said testily.

"Maybe so," Calno said, adding sarcastically, "Maybe the jet lag gave me brain damage."

Alper quenched his thirst with a one-gulp martini, then explained how instead of a likeness of Ralph Calno, Byrne had given Schwarz and Lyons an IdentiKit description based on the mug shot of a North Las Vegas man who'd been arrested for rape in Henderson the day before Vincent Hobbs's stolen Colt Cobra had been used to slay the security guard at Global Imports's downtown warehouse. The investigative report of the two field officers working on the burglary case had likewise been doctored to make it look as if the meter man Leila Yanders had seen outside Hobbs's trailer was this same rapist, no doubt on the prowl for lone women rather than stray handguns. It had taken Byrne the better part of seven hours of combing intrastate computer data banks before he'd stumbled upon the rapist, whose modus operandi consisted of posing as a telephone repairman when trying to gain access to his victims' homes. A perfect fall guy.

Of course, Byrne hadn't bothered to mention to Schwarz and Lyons that the man depicted by the composite was already in custody down south. With any luck, the two men would waste a few days on their wild-goose chase before stumbling onto that tidbit, and once they saw that the rapist had been caught prior to the warehouse murder, the theory that he had stolen Vincent Hobbs's gun would weaken considerably. If anything, the cover-up was specifically designed to bolster the circumstantial evidence by which Byrne and Alper hoped to eventually "prove" that Billy Hobbs had taken his uncle's gun and committed the murder for which he'd been killed while resisting arrest.

"Sounds well and good," Calno said. "But what if they check with that broad and find out the guy in the composite doesn't look nothin' like me?"

"That's not going to happen," Burlington promised.

"How can you be so sure?"

Alper interjected with obvious relish, "The same way you're sure Max Ernst isn't going to play tweety bird when Bobby goes back on trial."

"Ahh," Calno purred. "I see. Why didn't you say so in the first place?"

"Can we get onto other business?" Burlington interjected. Lowering his voice, he went on, "What the three of us need to concern ourselves with is protecting our interests against some supposed allies who have it in for us."

"Fries?" Calno guessed.

"And Kennesey," Burlington said. "Possibly Farrow, too. The way I hear it being talked up, once Bobby's back in the picture, they want to bump me out and replace me with their own people. I don't think I need to tell you where you two will stand if things line up that way."

"Damn!" Calno swore.

"It's all right," Alper said. He sipped some of his martini, then continued, "We're working out a plan that should take care of them nicely."

"I SUPPOSE we should get a copy of this composite sent back to the Farm," Schwarz said as he stared at the bogus IdentiKit form and burglary report he and Lyons had received from Lieutenant Byrne. "Who knows, maybe Bear can go fishing with it and reel something in.''

"Seems like grasping at straws, but at this point I'm willing to try anything," Lyons muttered, turning the Nova onto East Fremont. His frustration got the better of him and he slammed his fist on the dashboard. "Damn it, Pol, where are you!"

"Something tells me he's with Farrow," Schwarz said, mustering as much hope as possible into his voice, although he was as concerned as his partner about the fate of Blancanales.

Two police cruisers appeared in Lyons's rearview mirror, drawing closer by the second. When their rooftop lights began flashing, Ironman pulled over to the curb.

"All right!" he exclaimed. "Maybe they've got a lead!"

The cruisers, however, sped past without the officers inside so much as looking at the two men in the Nova.

"Then again," Schwarz grumbled, "maybe they haven't."

As Lyons eased back onto the road, he told Gadgets, "I've got to say, through all this shit that's comin' down, I smell a turf war brewing."

Schwarz let out an involuntary laugh. "That's got to be the most convoluted metaphor I've heard all week."

"Spare me the English lesson, Homes," Lyons snapped. "I've seen this scenario too many times before. You get a sense for it. There's a power struggle going on here, and Bobby Sumur's people are only on one end of it."

"I'll go along with that," Schwarz said. "But I don't know how much more we can do about it."

"It would have helped if we could have hauled in at least one of those skinheads for questioning."

"Hey," Schwarz snapped, "it wasn't like I really had the option of not shooting to kill back there at Farrow's."

"That's not what I meant. I just wish we could have knocked one of their wheels out of commission long enough to nab the drivers." They were coming up on the trailer park and Lyons flicked on his turn signal. "I know these white power punks think they're tough stuff when they're in gangs, but if we could get one or two of them alone for a little friendly persuasion, they'd squeal like pigs."

"Yeah, well, if wishes were horses . . . hey, what's this?"

Driving through the park to Hobbs's trailer, Schwarz and Lyons noticed that the two police cruisers that had passed them were parked next door, in front of the Yanders place. A paramedic's van was there as well, parked in the driveway. Gathering along the curb and front lawn was a crowd of curiosity seekers half the size of the mob that had viewed the marital fracas the other night.

Lyons parked in Vincent Hobbs's carport and the men got out of the Nova, crossing over to the Yanderses' property just as paramedics were emerging from the trailer hauling a stretcher containing a zipped-up body bag. Three cops came out next, surrounding the burly form of Richard Yanders, whose hands were cuffed behind his back. His face was flushed with tears as he looked at the body bag being loaded into the van.

"Leila!" he sobbed. "Leila!"

"Come on, pal, she can't hear you," one of the cops told him, prodding him toward the patrol cars. "You saw to that but good."

"I didn't do it!" Richard screamed with rage, turning on the officer. The other two cops quickly moved in to immobilize their prisoner and hustle him past observers into the back of the nearest car. All the while Yanders continued to proclaim his innocence.

"What happened?" Lyons asked one of the paramedics, taking care to show his federal agent's badge so he wouldn't get the runaround.

The attendant shook his head grimly. "Man, you don't wanna see," he said with conviction. "You don't even want to *know*."

"Guess again," Lyons said, following the man as he went to get back in his van.

As he started up the engine, the paramedic looked hard at Lyons and told him, "She was chopped up with an ax and stuffed in the fireplace, okay?" Glancing over at Yanders, he added, "Guy's putting on quite a show, the bastard. Sure he didn't do it! My ass."

Most of the trailer park residents shared the paramedic's sentiments, and once word of the nature of the murder spread through the throng, people crowded around the car taking Yanders away, waving fists and shouting epithets. Standing back, Schwarz and Lyons watched the ugly scene with mixed emotions.

"And to think we went to all that trouble to keep him alive the other night," Lyons muttered.

"Seemed like the right thing to do at the time," Schwarz said. "But maybe he's telling the truth."

"Go on," Lyons scoffed. "You're kidding, right?"

Gadgets shook his head. "Think about it, Ironman. She's probably the only person who got a good look at the guy who stole Hobbs's gun, and it's open season on witnesses around here, in case you hadn't noticed. What better method of getting her out of the way than to make it look like the old man went off his nut again?"

Lyons thought it over as they went back to Hobbs's trailer and let themselves in. "Yeah," he finally conceded. "You got a point."

Schwarz didn't answer his friend. He walked into the kitchen and stopped, staring at the half-cooked omelet left in the frying pan on the stove. He called out Vinnie's name as both he and Lyons drew their guns. They split off in different directions, cautiously checking the patio and all the rooms. When they caught up with each other in the den, Lyons kicked the sofa in anger. "What the hell's going on around here?" he shouted.

16

There was a relatively barren spit of land between North Main and Interstate 15 just south of the North Las Vegas city limits. The Union Pacific tracks ran through the heart of this wasteland, past the Las Vegas Indian Colony, where descendants of the city's original Paiute settlers were crammed into one of the smallest parceled reservations in the nation. There were a few other buildings scattered on the hardpan, most of them storage facilities or industrial shops like those closer to the downtown area.

Ned Farrow emerged from the rear doorway of one such building, the North Main Gun Club, a rectangular prefab structure four weeks away from its grand opening. He walked across the back parking lot to where his Mustang convertible was parked next to a trash Dumpster filled with broken bits of plasterboard and acoustic tile. The only other two vehicles in the lot were a pale gray Dodge station wagon and a Chevy Nova, both of them bearing visible signs of their recent collision along the back roads near Duck Creek.

Opening the trunk of his Mustang, Farrow bent over and pulled out the cage containing a Gila monster he'd finally managed to trap in the wash behind his home late the previous afternoon. The creature was two feet long, with a broad, flat face and small eyes that sparkled like polished gems before it closed them to block out the daylight sun. Its thick, stout body was covered with beadlike scales of black, yellow and orange-pink, lining up in vertical bands.

"Come along, my little monster," Farrow whispered to the creature as he lugged it back inside the building.

Set up primarily as a target range for gun enthusiasts, the building was soundproofed, and most of its space was set aside for the two dozen sectioned-off gallery lanes, where future members would be able to line up, don their earplugs and blast away to their hearts' content with the guns of their choosing.

For the present, however, there were only two gunmen taking practice. B.L. and Kenny Simms stood side by side behind the railings, loading more ammunition into their .357 Magnums.

"One more time, assholes," B.L. called out as he readied his weapon and assumed a firing stance. "Where's Billy Hobbs and how much do you know about what's going down with the syndicate here in Vegas?"

"What's that?" Blancanales shouted back at them from the target area of B.L.'s gallery. "I'm going a little deaf with all the shooting, you know?"

Blancanales, like Vincent Hobbs in the lane next to him, was tied to a chair situated directly below a bull's-eye target thirty yards down from where the Simms twins were taking aim with their Magnums. Both targets had been perforated countless times around the bull's-eye area, but some shots had strayed lower, to within inches of the captives' heads.

"Talk!" B.L. squeezed his trigger, sending a .357 slug whistling past Blancanales's ear. "Or maybe you want us to tape the targets to your chests?"

"Sure, why not?" Pol responded calmly. "See, fellas, the whole way you've gone about this is wrong. Vince and I know there's no way you're going to let us out of here alive, so why should we help you out? Think about it."

"Smartass!" B.L. shifted his aim slightly, sending a bullet through Blancanales's shirtsleeve and grazing his shoulder. Pol grimaced with pain and jerked slightly from the sting of the bullet's impact. Blood began to flow from the flesh wound, soaking his shirt. "Okay, so you're gonna die," the Simms brother told him. "You can decide whether it'll be fast or slow. Think about *that*!"

"Yeah," Kenny Simms added, aiming at Vincent Hobbs's ribs. "And think about how we're giving you more of a chance than you gave our sister!"

"Hobbs had nothing to do with that," Pol protested, but Kenny's Magnum blammed and Vincent groaned as the slug ripped into his side. As with B.L.'s shot, the bullet stung and drew blood without causing any life-threatening damage to its human target.

"Okay, ease up," Farrow called out as he joined the twins. "Let's not waste any more ammunition on them. I've got a little interrogation specialist to help us out."

"Whoa," B.L. said as he glanced at the Gila monster. "Heavy duty."

"B.L., grab that roll of mesh and bring it up with you," Farrow said as he climbed over the railing, still holding on to the Gila cage. He turned to the other twin. "I got to thinking while I was out back. If Billy

Hobbs is hurting as much as I think he is after I nailed him, he might have turned up a hospital or trauma center somewhere. Get on the phone and make a few calls. Start with the places closest to that packing plant and work your way outward.''

"Good idea," Kenny admitted. "Hate to miss all the fun here, though."

As Kenny headed off for the office, B.L. grabbed the three-foot-wide roll of chicken wire Farrow had referred to, then passed it to the bounty hunter before scrambling over the railing and striding down to where the two prisoners were trying their best not to show signs of either fear or pain.

"The Gila usually picks on smaller prey," Farrow said nonchalantly as he set down the cage and began unrolling the mesh to create a fence encircling the two men, "but this poor fella didn't get to eat last night, so who knows?"

"Suckers are poisonous as hell, too." Simms laughed, holding the fencing steady for Farrow.

Jaws clenched against the burning pain in his shoulder, Blancanales looked down at the caged beast, which was pacing within its confines. The creature, perhaps drawn by the scent of fresh blood, turned its head upward so that it was looking back at Pol. Blancanales had looked death in the face countless times before and always managed to walk away, but this time he had doubts that he'd be so fortunate. Still, if he was going to die, he was determined that he'd go out the same way he lived, in control, a smile on his face. He'd just nut up and do it.

"Well, Gila darlin'," the Able Team warrior cooed to the beast, "save the last dance for me . . ."

"I APPRECIATE your concern, but I can't let myself be intimidated by the likes of them," Donna Alvarez told Schwarz and Lyons.

"At this point, lady, it's more a matter of letting yourself be killed than intimidated," Lyons told her, pacing impatiently in the back office of the rescue mission. Besides him and Schwarz, there were two other men in the room, federal agents dressed down in secondhand casual clothes so they would blend in as much as possible with the environment Donna Alvarez was working in. Lyons pointed to the Feds while he continued to address the woman. "I'm sure these guys are doing a top-notch job of guarding you, and who knows, maybe they've already thwarted a couple of attempts on you without even knowing it, just by being close by.

"But you have to realize that the stakes are rising, Donna. We just found out that Max Ernst…remember him from Bobby Sumur's first trial? Well, last night he wound up dead in a parking lot out in Atlantic City, along with a woman and a bodyguard. The official word is they were blown off a casino walkway, but privately we all know they got a push."

Schwarz added, "And we just found out a witness in another case linked to the Mob was killed just down the road from here, next door to Vincent Hobbs's trailer. A woman, butchered with an ax and thrown in her fireplace."

Schwarz had deliberately refrained from pulling any punches in the description of Leila Yanders's death, hoping to make a convincing point. The strategy worked. Donna's eyes widened in horror as she envisioned the grisly murder. Taking a step backward, she leaned against the edge of her desk for support. "My God..."

"Shit, pal," one of the Feds yelled at Schwarz, "do you really have to lay all this on her?"

"She has to know what she's up against," Schwarz countered. He turned back to the woman. "Look, we admire your courage in wanting to go about your business, but considering all that's happening, you just have to temper that courage with a little wisdom."

Donna stared at the floor a moment, wrestling with her thoughts. "When you two got here," she murmured, "you said Pol couldn't be here because he was out working on another angle. Is he okay?"

"He knows how to take care of himself," Lyons said.

Donna glanced up at Lyons and Schwarz. "Something's happened to him, too, hasn't it?"

"We don't have any proof that—"

"Something's happened to him," she repeated with greater conviction. "And it's all because he got involved with me."

"That's not it at all," Lyons told her. "Yes, he's missing. So is Vinnie Hobbs, if you have to know. Damn it, Donna, can't you see we're trying to make sure you're not next?"

The woman stood back up and exhaled deeply. "Okay," she said. "What do you want me to do?"

Lyons gestured at the Feds again. "Let them take you to a safehouse. At least until some of this heat has died down. And if you can't see doing it just for yourself, think about those people coming in off the streets that you're trying to help. How would you feel if they got in the way of some attempt against you? Like that woman in Atlantic City?"

It was Donna's turn to pace the crowded room. She crossed her arms and bit on her lower lip. Through the door they could all hear the sounds of homeless men and women in the activity room, passing time, trying to make the best of this, their temporary refuge from the harsh life of the streets. Realizing now for the first time that she might be responsible for causing them a greater harm than what they were trying to avoid, her course became clear. She nodded to Gadgets and Lyons. "You're right, of course. I'm being selfish. I'll go."

"Good," Schwarz told her. "It's best, trust us."

"I do," she said. She took a key from her pocket and used it to unlock a desk drawer so she could get her purse. "Once you have some word on Pol, can you let me know?"

Lyons nodded. "Sure."

"I'm worried about him," she said. "And Vince."

"So are we," Schwarz said. "We're doing all we can to track them down."

Schwarz and Lyons fell in with the federal agents flanking Donna as she left the office. Two other bodyguards—just in town from Washington—were outside the building, trying to appear inconspicuous as they kept an eye on the street for suspicious activity. Once it was explained that Alvarez had agreed to go to a safehouse, the Feds split off into two cars, with Donna riding in the lead vehicle. She waved meekly to Lyons and Schwarz, who remained in the parking lot next to Lyons's rental Nova.

"Well, hopefully that's one less problem to worry about," Lyons said. "Now if we could just make some headway with the rest of this mess."

Lyons rummaged through his pockets for some change. "Let me call the station and see if Byrne or Alper have come up with anything."

"I'll check in with the Farm," Schwarz said, getting into the Nova as Lyons headed off for a pay phone located outside the mission.

Using his communicator, Schwarz linked up with headquarters in Virginia and asked to be put through to Aaron Kurtzman in the computer room. Bear sounded tired as he came on the line.

"Still fishing, Gadgets."

"Nothing yet?"

"Well, I'm pulling in all sorts of data, but I'm not really sure what we're specifically looking for, so it's hard to pinpoint, you know?"

"Okay, try this," Schwarz suggested. "You got a Vegas map in the computer?"

"Natch. Grid breakdowns, street index coordinates, you name it."

"Good. Try factoring in these things and see what you come up with." Schwarz closed his eyes a moment, sorting through his thoughts. "First off, chart all the ARC assault points."

"Already have that."

"Okay, now, did you run a check on addresses of all businesses owned by Global Imports?"

"Yes. No connection."

"What about Ned Farrow?"

"What about him?"

"You got him down as owner or partner in anything besides bounty hunting?"

"Let me check. Hold on."

As he waited, Schwarz stared out the windshield at Lyons, who had just slammed down the phone receiver and flipped his middle finger at it as he kicked the wall. Striding back to the Nova, Lyons got in and fumed. "Zip! They got nothing!"

"Shh, just a sec, Ironman," Schwarz interrupted, signaling for quiet as Kurtzman's voice came back over the small communicator.

"Ah, here's something. Seems Farrow's dropped some money into a gun club off North Main. Hasn't opened up yet, but—"

"Just give us the address," Schwarz said, starting up the Nova. "We're only a couple of blocks away."

17

Farrow stared at the two bleeding prisoners. "Sure you don't want to change your minds?"

"Forget it," Vincent Hobbs said. "Go ahead and kill me. Maybe it'll help make sure you get the chair when they catch you."

"Seems to me you're the one who's got the chair." Farrow chuckled. "You and the beaner over here."

Of the two captives, Blancanales had by far the more serious gunshot wound; he was weakening by the second from the loss of blood. Still, he tried his best not to show either his pain or his failing grip on consciousness. He kept watching the Gila monster, which was still in its cage only a few feet away. Farrow had half opened the latch a few seconds before, then closed it when the lizard tried to get out. To his right, Blancanales could see Kenny Simms fastening the ends of the wire mesh together so the makeshift fence would confine the Gila's dietary selection to the two prisoners once it was released.

"You ought to take this setup to the networks, Farrow," Pol managed to joke. "Work out a few bugs and you've got the makings of a great game show."

"I'm not playing games," Farrow told Pol. "You guys come up losers, you aren't going home with a year's supply of frozen fish dinners."

"Aw, gee," Blancanales whined. "I was counting on that."

"You want to count," Farrow taunted, leaning over the mesh and grabbing the latch to the lizard's cage. "I'll give you and Hobbs to ten to start talking, then it's dinner time."

"Fine," Hobbs said, calling Farrow's bluff. "I'll start. Ten..."

"Nine," Blancanales pitched in. Both men stared their tormentors in the eyes, resolving to be defiant to the end.

"Eight," Kenny Simms shouted, standing back from the wire enclosure.

"Seven," Hobbs and Blancanales cried out in unison.

As quickly as it had begun, the countdown was abruptly halted when B. L. Simms burst out of the office and shouted, "Bingo!"

Farrow and Kenny Simms both glanced back down the firing lanes to the railing, where B.L. appeared, looking euphoric.

"What did you find out?" Farrow demanded.

"Billy Hobbs is in postop at University Medical Center," B.L. told him. "Just got out of surgery. They say he's in satisfactory condition."

Farrow stood up, walking away from the unopened Gila cage. A fiendish smile crept across his face. "Is that a fact?" he said. "Well, he won't be in satisfactory condition for long."

As the bounty hunter strode away from the prisoners, Kenny asked him, "Hey, wait! What about these guys?"

Farrow told the brothers, "You're the ones with the grudge against the spic. He's all yours. I want the bastard that bashed my face."

Kenny looked at Blancanales and Vincent Hobbs, grinning sadistically. "All right!"

"Just clean up any evidence when you're done," Farrow told the brothers. Pointing at the prisoners, he said, "Once the lizard's had its fill, toss what's left of them into those big gunnysacks in the back room and we'll haul them out to the desert so the coyotes can fight for the leftovers."

"Sounds good to me," B.L. said as he leaped over the railing and joined his brother. The two of them stared at the prisoners, eyes filled with a mixture of hatred and malicious expectation. Neither spoke until they heard Farrow slam the back door behind him as he left the building, then Kenny aimed his .357 at Blancanales's face.

"One of your partners killed two of our buddies a couple of hours ago," he said.

"I'm sure he had his reasons," Pol responded evenly. "You think that killing us will bring them back?"

"No, but it sure as shit will make us feel a little better."

"And we already owe you for our sister," B.L. said.

Blancanales frowned. "Sister?"

"Claudette Simms," Kenny told him. "Or maybe you knew her as Mae Jung."

Blancanales took another look at the twins. All along he'd been bothered by a familiarity about them that he hadn't been able to pinpoint. Now that the connection had been made, he tried to play off it. "She had a gun to *my* sister's head," he told them. "She didn't give me any choice."

"Shut up!" Simms shifted his gun at the last second, firing a blast that splintered wood off the backrest of Pol's chair. While the shot reverberated through the range, B.L. stepped over the mesh and strode forward, lashing out with the barrel of his gun, pistol-whipping Blancanales across the head with so much force that Pol was knocked to the floor. Blancanales closed his left eye, feeling a numbness spread across the whole side of his face. The twin spit at him and kicked him in the ribs. "You killed her."

"Leave him alone!" Hobbs shouted.

Simms whirled around and pressed the tip of his Magnum against the soft flesh beneath Vincent's jaw. "You shut your fucking mouth unless you got something useful to say."

"Hey, come on, B.L.," Kenny called out to his brother from the other side of the fence. "Leave something for the lizard, why don't you?"

B.L. slowly backed away from the prisoners and stepped over the mesh to rejoin Kenny. "Okay, okay. Let's do it."

Kenny leaned over and unlatched the cage door. Perhaps daunted by the gun blast, the Gila monster was at first reluctant to move. It curled back in the corner of its cage, looking more serpentine than lizardlike. Kenny dragged the tip of his .357 along the sides of the cage, making a dull twanging sound.

"Get it in gear, damn it!"

The Gila finally responded, straightening itself and slithering through the cage opening. Its movements were slow but deliberate. Its head wavered to and fro, responding to cues from a highly developed sense of smell.

Lying sideways on the floor, Pol was at eye level with the beast, and from that lowered perspective the creature seemed even more loathsome and threatening than it had when he was sitting up. Blood from his shoulder was now flowing down onto his face, over the swollen cheek and stinging his eyes. He blinked to clear his vision and saw the monster crawling his way, exposing the grooved teeth in its powerful jaws, which were filling with poison secreted from salivary glands. Less than one-sixth of an ounce of the potent poison was enough to slay a man, and it would be released in the act of biting.

"Ave Maria, gratia plena," Blancanales whispered under his breath, instinctively recalling the favorite prayer of his childhood, back in the time when he had truly believed in divine intervention.

Dragging its thick body across the floor, the lizard crept closer to Blancanales, looking more like a messenger from Satan than the Blessed Virgin.

Still closer it crept.

"...dominus tecum..."

And closer.

When the creature was less than a foot from Blancanales there was a sudden popping sound, like the loud cracking of distant knuckles. The Gila monster jerked in place, as if it were a puppet whose master was caught up in a sneezing fit. Reptilian blood began to drain through its pebbly skin as it contorted and thrashed on the floor. There was another pop, and the lizard twitched a final time, then lay still on its side, revealing ruptures in its flesh where .45-caliber slugs had permanently spoiled its appetite.

"Freeze!" Carl Lyons shouted from the far end of the target range.

The twins glanced back and saw both Lyons and Schwarz standing behind the railing, still locked in the firing positions from which they'd unleashed the marksmanlike cross fire that had saved their partner from falling victim to the poisonous lizard.

"How'd you get in here?" Kenny Simms gasped in stupid wonder.

"We got invites to become charter members in the gun club," Lyons retorted. "You want another demonstration why?"

Kenny hesitated, but B.L. leaped into action, vaulting the mesh fence. Schwarz fired a shot his way, nicking B.L. in the thigh but failing to bring him down before he could take cover behind Vincent Hobbs.

"Drop your guns or he gets it," B.L. demanded, pointing his .357 against the back of Hobbs's skull.

"Don't listen to him," Hobbs insisted. "Take care of them!"

There was a momentary standoff. Lyons and Schwarz kept their guns aimed at Kenny Simms, whose Magnum was pointed at the ground. Kenny slowly shifted his aim until the barrel was lined up with Blancanales's head, then he grinned and laughed. "Looks like we're all gonna die, huh?"

"What'd be the point of that?" Schwarz bartered. "You guys can turn yourselves in, maybe turn state's evidence against Farrow and whatever Mob people you're involved with, the—''

''No way!'' Kenny snapped. ''We don't squeal to save our necks! You can kill us and our friends, but there's more of us out there to take over.''

Although he was bound to his chair, Vincent Hobbs had his feet on the floor, and as he witnessed the standoff he forced himself to be calm and tried to focus all his concentration on the youth behind him. Once he sensed that Kenny was dropping his guard slightly, Vincent pushed back on the chair with all his might, ducking his head sharply to his right in the same movement. Knocked off balance, B.L. fell backward, firing a wild shot that buried itself in the acoustical tile of the ceiling.

The distraction drew Kenny's attention momentarily, and Lyons took advantage of the break, squeezing off a shot that struck the twin in the chest. Kenny staggered against the mesh fence and swung around to fire back, but Lyons hammered him with another blow from his .45 and he toppled over the fence, landing on top of the slain lizard, inches away from Blancanales.

Schwarz, meanwhile, drew bead on B.L. as Vincent rolled clear of the twin. When B.L. tried to come up firing, Gadgets shot to kill. Five shots, five hits.

Then an eerie calm settled over the target range.

Lyons and Schwarz climbed over the railing and strode to the target area, guns still in hand in case either twin was only playing possum. When it was clear that both B.L. and Kenny were dead, they helped the two prisoners up and began untying their bonds.

''You've lost a lot of blood, amigo,'' Lyons told Blancanales.

"A fresh quart of thirty-weight and I'll be fine," Blancanales muttered as he stared down at his bleeding shoulder. "I don't know how the hell you found us, but *gracias*. That Gila was looking at me like I was headcheese," he told Lyons.

As Vincent was being untied, he asked Schwarz, "Did you get Farrow on the way in?"

"No," Schwarz said. "He was here?"

"You must have just missed him," Vince said urgently. "They found out Billy's at University Medical Center. Farrow's on his way there to finish him off!"

"Damn!" Schwarz looked around the unfinished range. "Where's a phone?"

"There's an office down the back hall," Blancanales said.

"I'll call the cops," Lyons said, breaking into a run down the firing lane. "They're just down the street from the hospital. Hopefully they'll be able to beat Farrow there."

18

Billy Hobbs dreamed that he was back in prison for the first time, still a teenager, only beginning to comprehend the magnitude of the consequences he was now forced to endure because of one night of drunken misjudgment. So many strong sensations. The coarse feel of the prison clothes against his skin, especially the chafing of the collar against his neck, always leaving a red, splotchy rash. The unsettling, unfamiliar smells of his new environment—strange body odors, mildew, vomit, urine, all mingling with and overpowering the weak pine scent of cheap disinfectant. The darkness of the cell after lights out and the soulless silence that came with it. Everyone watching him during the day, always with that knowing look, making him feel naked. The leers in the showers that first night when there was grappling, foul breath in his face, hands pinning him to the cold tiles of the floor, facedown.

And that had only been the beginning, a primer of what was to follow. Roll with the punches, try to keep track of the time, see an end somewhere down the line. Endure anything, everything, just don't give them any reason to keep you inside any longer than your sentence. Lap up the humiliation and be humble, show that you haven't been hardened, that you've been rehabilitated. Keep thinking good behavior, good behavior. Time off for good behavior. Then one day they unlock the cage and you're free. Back to society. Go and sin no more. Toe the line. Stick to your parole. Never going back. Never.

"Never," he whispered through his bruised lips, shaking off the dream but still clinging to the essence of its message. "I'm never going back."

"William?"

A woman's voice. He opened his eyes.

It was a nurse, not much older than he was. Pretty face, thin. Nice blond hair. Looks a little like Connie Newton, senior prom queen. He'd had a crush on her, thought about her often while in prison. High school. How many years ago was that? A lifetime ago.

"William?" she repeated, coming closer to the bed. "Are you awake?"

He nodded slightly. Feeling strange. Am I still dreaming? Am I dreaming of Connie?

"You came through surgery with flying colors," she told him as she took a syringe from a silver tray beside the bed. "The doctors are very encouraged. Except for some scarring, you should heal fully."

Billy tried to sit up and let out a groan as he became aware of the pain that enveloped him, especially around the area where he'd been shot.

"It's going to hurt for a long time, I'm afraid," the nurse said, swabbing his upper arm with cotton and readying the syringe for an injection. "This will help some."

He closed his eyes, barely feeling the needle pierce his skin.

"You're probably starving, aren't you?" the nurse asked.

"Yeah." His tongue felt thick, swollen. He turned his head, saw himself in a mirror on the wall. He was half-wrapped in gauze from the shoulders down, like part of a mummy. Face black and blue. "I look like shit."

The nurse blushed. "The swelling and discoloring will go down gradually over the next week or two. Now, I'll go see about some supper." She paused, weighing a decision. "I know you probably don't feel up to it, but there's a police officer here who needs to speak to you. The doctor said he can talk with you, but only for a few minutes, okay?"

Billy nodded grimly. "Guess from here they'll haul me to the prison infirmary."

"You won't be moved until you're strong enough," the nurse promised. No attempt to deny that he was bound for jail again. Think fast, Billy.

"My uncle," he mumbled. "Did you reach my uncle?"

The nurse nodded. "He said he'd be here a while ago, but he must have gotten held up in traffic. I'm sure he'll be here soon."

"I want a lawyer," he said, thinking more clearly by the second, rallying against the sedatives and pain-killers in his system. Never going back. "Tell the police I said that. I won't talk to them without a lawyer."

"I'll tell them."

"Now," Billy insisted. "Tell them now."

"Yes, yes, I will." She placed a hand on his forearm. "Now just lie back and don't get yourself all rattled. I'll talk to the officer, then I'll see about that food.''

"Thank you.''

The moment the nurse was out the door, Billy threw off his covers. He was linked by a long clear tube to a hanging sack filled with nutrient solution, primarily as a means of keeping a vein tapped in case there was need for an immediate injection of something more potent than mere painkillers. He grimaced and pulled out the needle, then pressed his hand against the trickle of blood as he got out of bed. One step and he almost fell to the floor.

Steady, Billy. Slow and steady.

He leaned back against the bed, taking a long, deep breath, gathering his strength. The nutrient solution dangled from a mobile stand. He used it for a crutch to get to the closet near the bathroom. His clothes, soiled, torn and rank, were wadded up in a plastic hospital bag along with his shoes. He changed as quickly as his limited stamina would allow, then eyed himself again in the mirror. He still looked bad, but he'd seen men roaming the streets in worse condition. He checked his pocket. Still had some spare change and a dollar bill he'd found on the street.

Going to the doorway, he eased the door open and peered out. He couldn't believe his luck; there was no cop guarding his room. He waited for an orderly with an armload of towels to pass, then ventured out into the corridor, hurrying to another doorway that led to the steps. Once inside the stairwell, Billy leaned against the nearest wall, gasping for breath. A huge 2 was painted on the opposite wall. Thank God, only one floor to descend, he thought. He felt faint. A cold sweat broke across his forehead and stars began to float about the periphery of his vision. He slumped down, sitting on the uppermost step leading to the ground floor, and put his head between his knees.

"Don't black out," he told himself. "Get a grip."

NED FARROW GLANCED UP as the nurse appeared in the doorway of the otherwise deserted waiting room.

"He's up now," she told him.

"Good," Ned said, rising from his chair.

"He's very weak and kind of upset," the nurse said. "I have to insist that you only stay a few minutes, like the doctor advised."

"Fine," Farrow said, walking beside the woman as they headed down the hall. A few minutes was all he'd need. It didn't matter how weak the kid was, there'd be a way to rig things up to make it look like he'd tried to attack Farrow. Yeah, poor bastard knocked me down and tried to grab my gun. Had to defend myself, didn't I? Of course, if some cop besides Byrne or Alper showed up first afterward, things might be a little sticky as far as him using his bogus ID to get to the room, but he could weather a little heat. It'd be worth it to have the kid shut up once and for all.

"I'll need to speak to him alone, of course," Ned told the nurse as they were coming up on Billy's room. "Standard procedure."

"That's fine," the nurse said. "I have to go get his supper and tend to my other patients. But I'll be back in five minutes and that will have to be all for tonight, okay?"

"No problem," Ned insisted. "Thanks for the cooperation."

"Glad to help." The woman hesitated a moment, then added, "I have to say, though, he seems like a nice boy."

"He's had all the fight knocked out of him for the time being, that's all," Farrow assured her.

"You're probably right."

The nurse headed off down the corridor. Farrow grinned to himself and opened the door to Billy's room. This was going to be a piece of cake. Or so he thought.

"What the hell!"

Seeing the vacant room, Farrow spun around and reentered the hallway, shouting at the nurse, "Is this your idea of a joke, lady?"

The woman looked back at him, confused. "What do you mean?"

"I mean there's no one in this room, goddamn it!" Farrow raged, unbuttoning his coat for quick access to his Casull .454. "Call security and have them watch the exits! That bastard's trying to escape!"

Scanning the corridor, Farrow gauged the likeliest escape route and stormed the stairwell. If he could corner Billy in there, things could still work out. Gun him down with no witnesses and it'd be his word against no one's. *Hey, he was trying to get away. I had to do it.*

There was a small puddle of blood on the steps. Farrow followed it, but the drops ceased halfway down. As he charged out of the stairwell into the main lobby, he looked around wildly. No sign of Billy. The security guards had been notified, but they could only shrug their shoulders to indicate they hadn't seen Billy leave the hospital.

Out in front of the building there were two police cruisers. Lieutenant Byrne was standing beside one of them, talking to an elderly woman in a wheelchair. Farrow went out to see him. From the expression on Byrne's face, he knew the bottom line before the lieutenant even spoke.

"She says he left in a taxi about ten seconds before we got here...."

19

Clint Dirry was between a rock and a hard place.

Even though Vegas Bobby Sumur had never been officially linked to the Caravan Hotel and its casino operations, the unsubstantiated rumors had been widespread enough to have forced a change in both ownership and management shortly after Sumur's sentencing to Carson City three years ago. Appointed public relations manager for the Caravan in the wake of that scandal, Dirry had devoted himself tirelessly in an effort to overcome the facility's tarnished image. He'd been responsible for arranging the countless charity functions hosted by the hotel and highlighted by hefty contributions by the Caravan itself. Dirry had also masterminded the establishment of several collegiate scholarship programs tying in with the high-tech needs of defense contractors working at nearby Nellis Air Force Base and Nuclear Testing Grounds. And he'd even struck a blow for detente by having the Caravan pick up the tab for a team of Soviet scientists who had come to Nevada as part of a mutual observation pact after the two superpowers had agreed to let a chosen few of their laboratory elite tour and inspect each other's nuclear weapons facilities.

Altruistic as these ventures might have seemed, in essence they merely served their intended purpose of falsely assuring both the general public and the Caravan's public stockholders that all Mob links with the casino/hotel complex had been severed when Sumur was sentenced. One of the benefits of the protracted trial that had led to Sumur's initial conviction had been that the Securities and Exchange Commission, the FBI and the three other agencies responsible for cracking the case, had been forced to spell out how they had brought Sumur down. Although witness testimony from the likes of Donna Alvarez and Max Ernst had played an integral part in the prosecution's case, there was also a plethora of supporting evidence that centered around such more cumbersome matters as double accounting, shadow ownership and profit-smuggling overseas. These countless back room machinations had allowed the syndicate to wriggle past the supposedly impregnable obstructions set in its path during landmark legislation passed in the late sixties by lawmakers eager to eradicate the Mob blight from Vegas and the other gambling centers in the state.

Clint Dirry had pored over transcripts of the trial, making countless notes and working in conjunction with the new manager of operations Rick Fries—not to make sure that the Caravan was now Mob-free, but to ensure that any future ties with organized crime would be structured in such a way as to avoid detection and accountability. It was Dirry who had sniffed out James Alper as the likeliest liaison with the law enforcement community, a figure hopefully capable of smelling out any hint that the Caravan might again be falling under suspicion by the SEC or the Bureau. It was Dirry who had brought Wes Burlington and Janice Kennesey into the picture on behalf of Bobby Sumur, essentially to provide the same function as Sumur, but without the blatancy or flamboyance that had eventually led to Vegas Bobby's undoing.

And up until the past few months, the scenario had been playing itself out nicely. No big mistakes, no drastic moves that might draw the wrong kind of attention, plenty of good press and input into the universal objective of every casino and hotel in Vegas, regardless of ownership—to make the city as glamorous and enticing to the tourist trade as possible. And behind the scenes things had run with equally smooth grace. Money was flowing in all the right directions, the stock had risen healthily as more and more shares were grabbed up by supposedly unrelated investment companies that were, in fact, mere fronts behind which the main players were building their power base. The Caravan had become a model for future surreptitious takeovers, the first step in a grand master plan whereby the syndicate would once again flex its muscle in Las Vegas, this time with more legitimacy and less chance for intervention.

Or so the plan had been.

Now Dirry saw the whole scheme being undermined by infighting and the crass displays of violence and brutality that had driven organized crime out of Vegas in the first place. The past month he'd seen it in the papers with increasing frequency. Store bombings, ax murders, shoot-outs in the suburbs, racial vandalism. As yet the media hadn't begun linking all the incidents together with speculation about a Mob resurgence, but it would only be a matter of time. And in the meanwhile, the word around town was that tourism had already begun to taper off, almost overnight, in response to the headlines. Who wanted to go to Vegas seeking instant fame and fortune if it meant running the risk of being killed in some act of supposedly random violence?

Something had to be done, and soon.

When he got a call to meet with Wes Burlington at the Potosi Place Restaurant, Dirry figured this would be as good a time as any to present his case and put in his plea for more restraint by the other players hooked into the master plan.

Potosi Place was located southwest of town, far off the Strip and adjacent to the Tropicana Wash Wildlife Habitat. Done up in adobe style, the restaurant was named after the tall mountain to the west, clearly visible from the main dining room, where the Mormons who had established Las Vegas in 1855 had briefly mined for lead. Other views gave one calming glimpses of the desert or the back nine at the West Palms Country Club. Touted for its Continental menu and an extraordinary wine selection, Potosi Place was a gathering spot for the well-to-do who wanted a respite from the frantic pace and buzz of the nearby city.

Dirry found Burlington in the dimly lit bar area adjacent to the dining room. He wasn't alone. Ralph Calno and James Alper were sitting on either side of him in a corner booth that, like every table and booth in the establishment, was deliberately set away from earshot of other patrons as a concession to the nature of most conversations that tended to occur when the city's movers and shakers met. There was room for only one more person at the corner booth, and even as he went to join the group, Dirry felt a knot forming in his stomach. He had a sick feeling as to what, contrary to his expectations, the conversation was going to cover.

"Good of you to come," Burlington told the stocky PR man. "Especially on such short notice."

"Yeah," Dirry said noncomittally. Why couldn't he have seen this coming?

"Drink?" Burlington asked, reaching for the pitcher of martinis in the middle of the table.

Dirry shook his head.

"We'll just have a quick chat," Burlington said, refilling his glass, "then we'll have some dinner, okay?"

"It's your dime, Wes."

Calno lit a cigarette and spoke for the first time as he stared at Dirry. "You look like maybe you already ate and it didn't agree with you."

"I'll be fine," Dirry said. "Let's just get on with this, okay?"

Like a dime store clairvoyant, Burlington looked directly into Dirry's eyes, then said, "I think you're concerned about all this bloodshed that's been going on, Clint." At the spark of surprise in Dirry's eyes, Burlington laughed gently. "It's no secret. And you're not the only one concerned, believe me."

Dirry took a pack of matches from the table and idly fingered it as he eyed the three men before him. "And I assume that the four of us are going to do something about it."

"Perhaps."

"Any reason why the others aren't here?" Dirry asked rhetorically. His nerves were becoming more and more chafed by the second, and he found himself dropping his guard, throwing out words like a man jettisoning excess baggage from a sinking ship, without much scrutiny. "Seems Fries might want some say in this. And Kennesey."

"Well," Burlington said with a sigh, "the way we see it, that's part of the problem. Fries wants a little too much say these days, we think. So do Janice Kennesey and Ned Farrow."

"Meaning what?"

Alper spoke up. "Meaning the pie's getting sliced too many ways. It's time to thin the ranks. That plain enough for you?"

Dirry nodded. "And why am I so blessed to be among the chosen?"

"Because Bobby wants you," Calno said. "And he just talked with Burlington here last night by phone and wants to shift some allegiances."

"I've got connections back east to handle Kennesey's end of things," Burlington said. "We don't need her anymore, especially now that she's gotten an appetite for the pie."

"And what about Fries?" Dirry inquired.

"He's going to have to take the fall for all this killing in town," Alper said. "And all that business with the Aryan Right Coalition."

"It wasn't his idea," Dirry said. "At least not all of it."

"Maybe not, but we've put together enough evidence to make it look that way," Burlington said. "We've got it blocked out so Fries, Kennesey and Farrow will have their hands caught in every bad headline we've run up against in the past month, from this whole Billy Hobbs thing to the killing of Max Ernst and that Yanders woman."

"How?" Dirry wanted to know. "I mean, who's going to think that killing witnesses is somebody else's idea and not Bobby's?"

"Think about it, Clint," Alper suggested. "If you wanted to make sure Sumur stayed behind bars, you'd try to make it look like he was calling for those executions, right? We're painting it so Fries is behind it, because he wants to keep all the action he's taken over with Bobby out of the picture. He cozied up to Kennesey for financial backup and had Farrow bring in ARC as a hired rogue force to help stake out some new frontiers."

Dirry shook his head. "This is crazy. It'll never work. Never in a million years!"

"Maybe you weren't listening," Calno told him. "The trap's set. All we have to do is get those three to fall into it."

"And that, Clint," Burlington concluded, "is where you come in."

THE SAFEHOUSE Donna Alvarez had been taken to was located in a new housing development three miles west of the North Las Vegas Air Terminal but still within the city limits of Las Vegas proper. As with Ned Farrow's place on the other side of town, the safehouse was, for the time being, set off from the other completed homes, which were actually spaced apart to provide the first tenants with a temporary perk of added privacy.

Sitting inside the sparsely furnished living room, Donna stared out the back sliding door at the cement slab patio and the grassless lawn. In the distance, beyond the property walls, the Spring Mountains were red and fiery where the sun set behind them like a fireball dropping into a shallow caldron. A sudden feeling of sadness overcame her and she closed her eyes, fighting a losing battle against a sob lodged in her throat. It came out as a pained whimper, forcing a flow of tears from her eyes.

"Excuse me," she apologized to a female federal agent who had joined the security detail.

"That's okay," the woman assured her. Like Donna, she was wearing slacks and a light sweater. Over the latter she also wore a shoulder holster containing a Beretta automatic. There were two other agents in the house standing vigil near windows offering views of the more likely approaches to the building. Another man was outside, doing some gardening as part of his cover.

"You have a right to be upset," the woman reassured Donna. "If I was in your shoes I'd be crawling the walls."

"It's not just that," Donna confided, blinking away the tears and regaining her composure. Glancing around at the layout of the house, her voice quavered slightly. "My husband and I were planning to move into a small tract home like this. Up north near Regional Park. A beautiful place. We were going to get a dog, have a little garden area, maybe even a few citrus trees. The deal was in escrow when..." She couldn't bring herself to go on. Assailed by the sudden image of her husband lying dead in the back alley behind their nightclub, Donna curled slightly in her chair, bringing her hands to her face as the grief washed over her.

The other woman came a few steps closer and rested a hand on Donna's shoulder. "I'm sorry, Donna," she said. "I really am."

Donna was racked with sobs a few moments longer before the image passed and she was once again able to rein in her emotions. The agent handed her a tissue and she used it to dab her dampened cheeks. They were silent a while after that, and the house was filled with an eerie calm, punctuated by the soft sounds of the men shifting their stances in the other room and the agent outside pushing a wheelbarrow of mulch over to a flower bed near the driveway.

"The funny thing is," Donna finally said, "now that I've spent so much time down at the mission tending to the homeless, even a small place like this suddenly seems almost obscenely lavish. Do you know what I mean?"

The other woman nodded, going back to her post near the sliding glass door. "It's amazing how arbitrary some values can be when your perspective changes even the littlest bit."

Donna got up from her chair and walked over to a side window, from which she could see that the only other completed house in view was more than two hundred yards away. "How long will I have to be here?" she wondered aloud.

"Hard to say, I'm afraid," the agent told her. "Not too long, hopefully. We know it's a hardship."

"If it helps bring justice to the people who killed my husband and who are spreading all this hatred throughout the city, I can live with it."

"It takes a lot of courage to do what you're doing," the other woman said. "Most people these days would rather stick their head in the sand than take a stand on anything, much less something as important as—''

''Company,'' one of the men in the other room interrupted, going for his shoulder holster. He moved from in front of the den window to beside it. The other man strode across the floor to the front hallway, taking up position near the door.

The female agent reached for her gun as she spoke to Donna. ''Okay, it's into the cellar like we discussed.''

The agents acted with professional calm but Donna could still detect their intensity as they prepared to serve their function as her protectors. Even the man outside had abandoned his wheelbarrow and taken cover behind a waist-high retaining wall, from which position he had a clear view down the driveway to the unpaved road running past the small home.

Donna had opened a door leading down to a small subterranean enclosure and started down the steps when the man near the front window relaxed and called out, ''False alarm. They're with us.''

Donna retreated from the steps, a look of hopeful expectation on her face. ''Is it the three men from Special Forces?''

''Three? I count four.''

Donna went into the den and looked out the front window as the Nova pulled into the driveway. Lyons and Schwarz got out of the front, then Gadgets opened the back door and helped Blancanales exit the back seat. Pol's left arm was in a sling, and even from the distance Donna could see how bruised and swollen the side of his face was. Nonetheless, when he spotted Donna watching him, he smiled and offered a wave with his good hand.

The fourth man was Vincent Hobbs, who handed a laptop computer out to Schwarz before exiting the car, moving stiffly and using crutches to ease the pain he felt in his rib cage each step he took. Donna opened the door to greet them. Her expression of relief turned to concern when she got a closer look at Blancanales's discolored face.

"What happened?" she gasped. "My God, you look awful."

"Flattery will get you everywhere," Pol said, chuckling as he negotiated the front steps. "There was this place on North Main offering free facials."

"It's not funny, Pol," Donna said, leading him into the den. "You must be in agony. And you're limping, Vince."

"Had my ribs tickled with a Magnum," Vincent deadpanned. "I'll survive."

"You should probably be in the hospital," she scolded both injured men.

"That's what they told us, too," Hobbs said, "but we didn't buy it. Too much going on to be stuck on the sidelines."

As Pol, Hobbs and Lyons sat down in the den and related their encounter with the Simms twins, Schwarz took the laptop into the closest bedroom, which was half-filled with a complex computer system that had been installed weeks ago for a non-related safehouse assignment involving a fraudulent stockbroker. Gadgets had already secured clearance to use the system. As he set it up, he explained to the agent watching him, "Once this baby's humming, hopefully we'll be able to run a check on all the local cab companies and find the driver who picked up Billy Hobbs when he left the hospital.''

"I'll believe it when I see it," the agent said skeptically. "Me, I don't put much stock in computers. Ain't natural."

Schwarz glanced up from the terminal. "Follow that logic and you should be toting a club instead of that Beretta in your shoulder holster."

The agent thought it over and shrugged. "Maybe so."

Outside, the sun slipped below the horizon, taking the last of the day's light with it. Lights were turned on inside the safehouse. Once the computer was ready for operation, Schwarz linked up the modem unit and began methodically working the keyboard. "I look at it this way," he told the agent. "I'm Aladdin and this is my magic lamp. I rub it the right way and my wishes are gonna come true."

ALTHOUGH RALPH CALNO, like Ned Farrow, was best known for his heavy-handedness, when the situation called for it, he could also be a master of finesse. During the dinner that had followed the men's discussion at the Potosi bar, for instance, Calno had excused himself briefly on the excuse of having to make a phone call, when in reality he slipped out of the restaurant to plant a small transmitter inside the cellular phone in Clint Dirry's Ford Fairlane. Then, back inside, he'd also seen to it that the Caravan's public relations wizard had a second, even smaller mike affixed to his portable pacemaker, a well-concealed concession to a hereditary heart malfunction. The latter plant had been far more difficult to arrange than the bugging of the car, but with the assistance of Burlington and Alper, the necessary distraction had been created and Dirry was tapped without realizing it.

Now, two hours later, as Dirry drove back to town following dinner, Alper and Calno followed from a safe distance in Calno's custom Jaguar. A receiver attuned to both Dirry's mikes rested on Alper's lap and the police sergeant fidgeted with both the tuning and volume knobs, monitoring every discernible noise inside the Fairlane.

"I got twenty bucks says he gets on his cellular before he reaches the Strip," Alper wagered.

"No bet," Calno said. "Unless you want to go odds on him spilling the plan."

Alper shook his head. "Nope. He's too smart to try crossing us. Has too much to lose going that route. No, he'll lay it out the way we planned."

"We'll see."

They didn't have to wait long. Dirry had driven no more than four blocks before he was putting a call through to Janice Kennesey. Despite occasional bursts of random static, Alper and Calno were able to make out all of the conversation.

"Hello?"

"Janice. It's Clint."

"Oh, hi, Clint. What's up?"

"We've got a problem."

"Serious?"

"Very."

"Just a second." There was a moment of silence, broken by the sound of Dirry clearing his throat, then Janice came back on the line. "Sorry, I just sent Phyllis out. You sound pretty uptight."

"I have reason to be uptight, Janice. I just found out there's an SEC probe brewing, and they've got their sights set on the Caravan."

"No..."

"Afraid so. I'm pretty sure we've got ourselves covered on all fronts, but they could still make things difficult for us, especially with all this stuff with Bobby's new trial."

"That's an understatement if there ever was one," Kennesey said. "This could be a disaster."

"But maybe not. I think there's a way to wriggle off the hook."

"How's that?"

"Well, I need to get together with you, Fries and Farrow to discuss it in detail, but basically I think we can frame Burlington so it'll look like all the guilt's on his shoulders."

"How?"

"Like I said, I'll have to spell it out in detail once all of us are together. Can you arrange it?"

"What am I, a social secretary?"

"Janice, I know you've got both those guys wrapped around your little finger. You can get them to jump to your tune by just snapping."

"What makes you say that?"

"Come on, Janice. I got eyes and ears. I pick up things here and there."

"Like what kind of things?"

"Don't turn me into a gossip monger, Janice, all right? Just play along with me on this one and I can make it worth your while."

"Okay, okay. What do you have in mind?"

"A meeting. Tonight. Ten o'clock. At your warehouse."

"Why there?"

"Well, the hotel's out for obvious reasons, and I'm sure Farrow's places are still being watched. You heard from him since that thing at the hospital?"

"Yes, I just talked to him. He's out cruising for Billy Hobbs. He's obsessed about getting that kid. I've never seen him like this."

"Well, make sure he gets unobsessed long enough to make this meeting. He's going to have to do his share to keep the noose off his neck."

"What's the plan, Clint?"

"I'll spell it out when we meet. It's complicated and I only want to have to go through it once."

"Well, I'll call Ned right back, then Fries. The warehouse at ten, right?"

"That's it. See you then."

"Okay. I hope this works."

"We play our cards right, it will. Later..."

Alper and Calno listened to Dirry hang up his phone, take a deep sigh, then turn up his car radio. Alper turned down the receiver and grinned at Calno. "He's following the script so far. Now we just have to hope she can get Farrow and Fries over to the warehouse with her."

"If she can reach them, they'll be there," Alper ventured. "They'll both jump at a chance to help themselves up the ladder and take Burlington out of the picture at the same time."

Calno chuckled. "I'm gonna love seeing the look on their faces when they realize the shoe's on the other foot." At the next intersection, he turned, powering the

Jaguar up Rainbow Boulevard. "By the way, just out of curiosity, who did that dice job on Leila Yanders? Farrow?"

Alper shook his head. "Byrne."

"Byrne? You got to be kidding."

"Nope."

"Whaddya know," Calno marveled. "I didn't think the bastard had it in him. Shit, I been at it a long time and I never axed somebody and threw 'em in a fireplace. Who gave him that idea?" Alper shrugged. "Beats me. Blood lust, I guess. Worked out nicely, though. Kinda seemed like something her old man would have done. Poor bastard'll never be able to convince folks it wasn't him."

"Byrne," Calno repeated. "I got to give him more credit."

"If you really mean it, you might want to lean on Bobby and Burlington, see if they can't cut him in for a better chunk," Alper suggested.

"With a little guidance he just might make a good capo at some point down the line."

"Good as you?" Alper asked.

"Fuck no." Calno laughed. "I'm the best!"

"And humble, too."

"Damn straight."

"How many people you figure you iced so far?"

"Those three in Atlantic City brought me up to thirty-four," Calno boasted. "A few more years and I'll be ready for the goddamn Guinness book. Most prolific hit man."

"Well, after tonight you should have three more at least," Alper said.

20

While Schwarz continued his computer search for the cabdriver who'd picked up Billy Hobbs outside University Medical Center, Lyons left Blancanales to have some time with Donna and drove the Nova back into town. He parked at the police station and entered the building with two pieces of business on his agenda. Both Alper and Byrne had the night off, so he had to postpone his plan to lay into them for their general ineptitude with regard to strike force activity. However, after pulling all the collective clout he could draw upon, he was able to make good on his second mission, to see Richard Yanders.

The man was in a solitary cell, wearing a prison uniform several sizes too small for his massive frame. He looked drained and defeated in the wake of his wife's death and his arrest for her murder, and when Lyons stated the primary reason for his visit, Yanders stared at him with a look of both skepticism and despair.

"You think I'm innocent?" he said mockingly. "Yeah, right."

"I mean it," Lyons insisted.

"Bullshit," Yanders shot back. "This is just some trick you're pulling, trying to throw me off my guard. Well, forget it. I didn't kill her and you're not going to trick me into a confession with some hocus-pocus reverse psychology, got that?''

Lyons sighed. He could understand the man's reluctance, given the circumstances. But he persisted, trying to break down the barrier between them. ''If you were the murdering type, you would have killed your wife the other night instead of putting on that show to let everyone know what a drunken idiot you could be when you put your mind to it. And after that performance, there's no way you'd turn around and kill her with the same ax and think you'd get away with it, right?''

The prisoner mulled over Lyons's words, looking as if he longed to believe them. Paranoia won out, however, and the sullen glower returned to his face.

''I still don't trust you, man,'' Yanders said. ''I ain't saying squat.''

''Okay, fine, be that way,'' Lyons said, ''but I think your wife was killed by the same guy she saw hanging around Vinnie Hobbs's trailer that day his Colt got swiped.''

Yanders's eyes narrowed as he took a long hard look at Lyons. This time his resistance cracked. ''You think so?'' he finally muttered.

Lyons nodded. ''I was hoping you might have some idea who that was. Did Leila mention anything about him . . . something she didn't tell the cops?''

Yanders thought about it, then shook his head. ''No. Not all that much to say. Just what he looked like, his excuse for being there. . . .''

''And he looked like this, right?'' Lyons reached into his coat and pulled out the composite given to him by Lieutenant Byrne. He handed it to Yanders, who looked at it for only a few seconds before glancing back up at Lyons.

"Okay, I give," he said. "You're screwing with me. I don't know why, but that's it. Where's my lawyer?"

"I just wanted to see if you remembered her giving any more description than she gave the cops."

"Look, pal," Yanders said, pointing at the composite. "That's not the guy Leila saw. What kind of fast one are you trying to pull on me?"

Lyons looked at the rendering, dumbfounded. "Well, then, what did she say the guy looked like?" he asked.

"Short, big ears, light hair and eyes," Yanders recalled. "Just the opposite of this guy here. I don't know who the fuck this is supposed to be."

"Must have been some kind of mixup," Lyons said. For him, some of the myriad pieces of the Vegas puzzle were at long last starting to fall into place. He excused himself from the cell long enough to track down an on-duty officer skilled with the IdentiKit. The two of them went back to Yanders, relying on his second-hand description of the man his wife had described as the meter man to put together a new likeness. The finished product looked nothing like the man depicted in the composite Lyons had been given earlier.

"Shit," he muttered as he stared at the new simulated mug shot. "I've seen this guy before."

Searching back through his cluttered memory, Lyons closed his eyes, trying to make the connection. Finally, just as he was about to give up, it came to him. Years ago, back when he was first with the Feds' Organized Crime Strike Force. Yeah, back then he'd gone up against this guy. He'd been just a gofer with one of the St. Louis families. Damn, what was his name?

"Calno," he finally blurted out, surprising himself. "Ralph Calno."

THE LITTLE MONEY Billy Hobbs had on him was only good enough for a mile's worth of cab fare, but that had gotten him back to the sanctuary of the packing plant, where he had taken refuge in the same upper-story room where he'd stayed prior to his confrontation with Ned Farrow the previous day. He figured no one would expect him to return here, and because most of the other transients were off in the food lines around sundown, Billy felt secure enough to give in to the fatigue eating away at him. Slipping quickly into a deep slumber, Billy found himself once again transported to that realm of troublesome dreams, and again he relived the terrors of his incarceration in Carson City. While he slept, the effects of his painkillers slowly wore off, and less than two hours later he was jarred awake by the burning ache in his shoulder. Agonizing as that sensation was, however, it was still preferable to the nightmarish images that had been tormenting his sleep.

Sitting with his back against the wall, Billy closed his eyes and rocked slowly back and forth, trying to focus his mind on something besides the pain. Back and forth. Run and hide. It seemed to him as if the torturous eternity of the past few days had been spent in a constant state of flight, and all of it undeserved. Whoever had framed him for that guard's murder had turned him into an embattled fugitive, and it was with rising anger that Billy finally found a place to channel all his pain and suffering. For him, the hurt began to serve as a reminder that he had been used, and he became equally certain that the only sure way of relief was to avenge himself and track down the party responsible for his dilemma. Under the right circumstances, revenge could be a powerful tonic, and for Billy Hobbs it served as his rallying point, his reason for going on.

Presently, he heard some of the other transients returning to the plant, conversing in their usual chorus of low murmurs as they staked out places to spend the night. Billy rose from the floor of his secluded chamber and trudged out onto the walkway, then down the stairs. Each step required a great effort and cost him dearly in pain, but he put one foot before the other and forged on. Once he reached the ground floor, he heard the voices of the others and could feel their eyes upon him, but he paid them no mind. They were of no concern to him. His destiny awaited him elsewhere.

"Hey!" someone called out to him as he approached the doorway. Billy pretended he didn't think the salutation was directed at him and continued toward the exit. Before he could reach it, however, the strongest transient in the group took a few long strides and blocked the opening. "I was talking to you, dude. You deaf or something?"

Yeah, Billy thought to himself quickly. I'm deaf. And dumb. He tried to shuffle past the tall man, who reached out and grabbed him by his wounded shoulder. Billy let out a ragged scream and the tall man drew away, shocked. Billy staggered through the doorway and outside.

"Somethin' about that guy's not on the level," the tall man grumbled to the others.

STOP ALONG any street corner on the Strip or Glitter Gulch, and if there's a row of newspaper vending machines, the odds are half of them will contain free handouts featuring photos of half-clad women in provocative poses, volunteering services ranging from escort or massage to nude modeling. Between the lines, however, there is an implicit availability of sex for hire. By and large, the arrangement came about as a way to provide an outlet for prostitution in Vegas without scaring off tourists who might blanch at the presence of hookers and pimps plying their trade in a less discreet manner. As it was, pimp-supervised streetwalkers like Ned Farrow's friend Annie were a rarity both on the Strip and off.

Lieutenant Byrne knew the nature of the Vegas flesh-peddling game as well as anyone, not from the perspective of a police officer but rather as a frequent customer of the innumerable outcall services provided primarily to male visitors anxious to indulge in vices other than those provided inside the glittering confines of the casinos. Once each week, Byrne would treat himself to a so-called jollies night, and over the months since he'd first instigated the practice, he'd become increasingly ritualistic about the way things would be handled. On the way home from work, he'd pick up every available flyer touting outcall services, then once inside the privacy of his condominium near the Showboat Country Club on Warm Springs Road, he'd clip out the various phone numbers and put them in his police cap, shake them up and pull out a lucky winner. From there, he'd proceed with several more random drawings to determine the ethnicity of the woman he'd call for and the nature of the sexual encounter he'd want to have with them when they showed up at his doorstep.

Tonight he'd chosen an outfit called Escortissima and had placed his request for an Asian woman specializing in domination. Arrangements made, Byrne then treated himself to a forty-five-minute bath in perfumed water and mineral salts as he sang along with a recording of the opera *Tristan und Isolde*. Then, after donning a complete Edwardian tuxedo over his scarlet bikini briefs, Byrne proceeded to the kitchen, where he put on an apron decorated with pictures of Julia Child and began setting out the ingredients for a gourmet meal he would prepare while his female consort would perform a striptease and do whatever else she could to tantalize him while he cooked, so long as she didn't touch him. He'd found this strange bit of foreplay to be one of the more arousing parts of the ritual, often surpassing the subsequent meal and later pleasures.

Byrne was still setting out ingredients for tonight's duckling *à l'orange* when the front doorbell rang. The lieutenant frowned with displeasure as he glanced at his wall clock. She was more than ten minutes early, damn her. He just hated it when they did that.

As he unlocked the door and started to open it, Byrne snapped, "I specifically said eight-thirty, and—"

"Gee, sorry, Lieutenant," Lyons said as he stiffarmed the door before Byrne could close it on him. He strode into the room, followed by Blancanales and Vincent Hobbs, whom he'd picked up on the way over. Schwarz was still working on the safehouse computers.

Looking at Byrne's tuxedo, Lyons said, "Hey, looks like you're all dressed up and nowhere to go, huh?"

"This is my night off," Byrne huffed, remaining near the door. "And I'm expecting company, so I'll have to ask you to leave."

"You've got more than just the night off, friend," Lyons told him.

Blancanales shoved the policeman away from the door and closed it, throwing the dead bolt. Hobbs glared at Byrne and suddenly lashed out with one of his crutches, prodding the cop against the wall.

"You're as low as they come," Hobbs spit at the man.

"What's the meaning of this?" Byrne demanded. "This is inexcusable!"

"I'll tell you what's inexcusable," Lyons told him, pulling out his Government Model .45. "What's inexcusable is when the boys in blue brownnose the men in the Mob."

"I don't know what you're talking about."

"Have a seat, Lieutenant," Blancanales suggested, pointing to an overstuffed chair in Byrne's living room. "We just want a little chat, that's all. No need to get upset."

Hobbs pulled his crutch away from the cop. Byrne's indignant facade began to crack. He warily crossed the room and sat down as Pol went over to the windows and drew the shades.

"Okay." Lyons laid out the ground rules as he plopped down on an ottoman and faced the lieutenant. "This is going to be like baseball. Man on third, two outs, bottom of the ninth. You get three chances to get on base with us by telling the truth. Three strikes, though, and you're out, but good. Understand?''

Byrne nodded feebly.

"Good, good," Lyons said. "First question. This little buddy-buddy bit with Ralph Calno and the Mob..,who besides you is cutting deals from the police end?''

"I don't understand.''

Lyons put it more succinctly. ''Who's on the take along with you, asshole?''

Byrne bit his lip, buying time. This was all happening too fast. ''What kind of slack do I get if I talk?'' he bartered.

"Who do I look like, Monty Hall?'' Lyons asked. "You talk, maybe you live. How's that?''

Byrne didn't have to think about it for long. He'd done his homework and knew that in their own way, the men of Able Team could be as merciless as Ned Farrow when the spirit moved them. ''It's just me and Alper,'' he muttered. ''At first it was just him, but I overheard something and he—''

"We can get into gory details later," Lyons interrupted.

"He's one for one," Blancanales said.

"And Farrow's in on it, too?'' Lyons asked Byrne. Byrne nodded.

"Two for two," Hobbs said.

"Very good," Lyons said. "Now, where are they? As we speak?''

"I don't know," Byrne said. "I swear, I don't know.''

Blancanales shrugged. ''Well, two out of three ain't bad.''

"Not for starters."

"Hey, you said just three questions," Byrne protested.

"Well, you just knocked in the tying run," Lyons said. "We're going into extra innings. There's so much more to know—"

The communicator clipped to Lyons's belt beeped. Keeping his eyes on Byrne, Lyons picked up the device. It was Schwarz calling.

"The driver who picked up Billy Hobbs took him to an old deserted packing plant by the U-P tracks," Gadgets reported.

"How far away is that?" Lyons asked.

"You're almost there," Schwarz told him, giving directions.

"We'll meet you there," Lyons said.

As Lyons signed off, Blancanales asked, "A lead on Billy?"

Lyons nodded, turning to Hobbs and handing him his .45. "How about you baby-sit the lieutenant until the Feds show up?"

"Glad to," Hobbs said, easing into a chair and aiming the gun at Byrne. "After all you put me and Billy through, buddy, you better not even breathe wrong."

21

After leaving the hospital and learning of the debacle at the shooting club, Ned Farrow had opted for the strategy of hiding in plain sight. Leaving his Mustang and trademark Stetson inside the multilevel parking garage behind the Imperial Hotel, he'd stopped by the gift shop for an "I Love Vegas" baseball cap before picking up a rental Thunderbird and once again cruising the streets of Las Vegas. He carried his Casull .454 and his portable cellular phone.

What a damn sorry mess it was all turning into, he mused bitterly as he wound through a quiet suburban neighborhood far from the glitter of the Strip. Up until a few days ago everything had been shaping up nicely, but beginning with that warehouse robbery he'd rigged, it had been one headache after another, and the more he tried to remedy the situation, the worse it seemed to get. Like struggling in quicksand; the more you tried to get out, the quicker you sank.

The phone buzzed as he was turning a corner. He picked up the receiver, saying nothing.

"Ned?" It was Janice Kennesey.

"Yeah?"

"I just talked with Clint Dirry."

"So?"

"You won't believe it! He's playing right into our hands without knowing it."

"What do you mean?"

"He's got a plan to take out Burlington and pin all the ARC and witness murders on him at the same time."

"What kind of plan?"

"He wants to meet with us to discuss it. Tonight."

"Who's 'us'?"

"You, me . . . and Rick Fries."

"What?"

"Look, Ned, I know we wanted to cut Fries out, too, but if Dirry's already got something lined up, that's gotta mean that Sumur's backing it, so that saves us having to stroke him. It's worth the price."

"I hate Fries," Farrow complained. "I don't want to have to go on pretending I don't."

"It would only be for a while, Ned, I'm sure. Hell, once we get the gears all rolling, we can see about getting Fries sent north, to Tahoe maybe, or Carson City. Or we leave him here and could go there ourselves. You know they've been saying all the real action is up there. There are all kinds of possibilities."

Approaching a retail strip, Farrow spotted a man hobbling along the sidewalk. He slowed down, reaching for his Casull. But it wasn't Billy Hobbs. "Damn . . ."

"Don't be like that, Ned."

"It wasn't about that," Ned said.

"Then can you come? At my warehouse. Ten o'clock."

Ned glanced at the dashboard clock. Forty minutes from now. "Okay," he muttered. "I'll be there."

"Good. It's all going to work out in our favor, Ned. Trust me."

"See you then." Ned hung up the phone and reached into his coat pocket, pulling out a handful of five-round speedloaders for his Casull. Their bulkiness was reassuring, like the feel of hot dice in the hands of a crap shooter. "I don't trust anyone but Ned Farrow," he whispered to the night.

FEDERAL SPECIAL AGENT Frank Boulam felt privileged to be riding alongside Gadgets Schwarz as they sped through town to the industrial quarter. During the three years he'd been attached to the roving Organized Crime Force, Boulam had heard countless legends involving Able Team, some of them prompted by envy, some by sheer admiration, and all of them painting a larger-than-life picture of three reckless shitkickers who made Rambo look like a schoolmarm in comparison. To have finally encountered them in the flesh during these past few days in Vegas was already an experience he would be talking about for years, and now he was in a position to actually accompany them on part of their most recent mission. It was all he could do to maintain a semblance of professional reserve and not betray the boyish enthusiasm that had his stomach squirming as if its butterflies wore boxing gloves.

"That must have been quite a firefight at that shooting gallery, huh?" he asked Schwarz with feigned nonchalance. "It looked like Blancanales took a real bad hit."

"Nah, that was just a scratch." Schwarz kept his eyes trained on the sparse traffic as he turned a corner and eased down on the accelerator. "He's taken worse and come back fighting."

"From what I hear, you all have," Boulam said. "I guess maybe we might be in line for some more tonight."

"Could be," Schwarz said. "That's why you're along for the ride, after all, right?"

"Right, right," Boulam said. The Beretta nestled in his shoulder holster suddenly felt heavier, and he began to wonder if the real cause for his uneasy stomach was the fact that in all his years of service he'd yet to fire his gun at a human adversary. There was no way he was going to own up to as much, especially to Schwarz. As it turned out, he didn't have to. Gadgets could sense the man's apprehension.

"Little nervous?"

"Just a little," Boulam confessed.

"It's natural," Schwarz assured him. "Means your reflexes haven't conked out on you. Just go with it, use it in your favor."

"You mean you still get nervous going into an assignment?" the younger agent asked.

Schwarz laughed. "Hell yes, I do. All that adrenaline's gotta come from somewhere."

"I guess you're right," Boulam said. "I never thought of it that way."

"Now might be a good time to start."

The old packing plant loomed up ahead in the distance. A Union Pacific train was on its way through Vegas on the nearby tracks, sounding its special thunder across the littered wasteland. Schwarz pulled off the main road and beelined toward the building, where he saw another vehicle just pulling up from the other direction. By the time he caught up with them, Lyons and Blancanales were already getting out of the Nova.

Once Schwarz had introduced the newcomer to his partners, Lyons gestured toward the nearby building. "Well, let's hope Billy's stayed put for once. Fan out and we'll take it from all sides, just to be safe."

Breaking off, the men cautiously circled the building and closed in on windows and doorways from which they could have a look inside. The rumbling of the train masked their movements, just as it had masked the approach of their cars.

Lyons crept up to the main entrance, holding his breath against the raw, foul stench from where too many men had used the side of the wall for a urinal. Through the doorway, he had a clear view of the main chamber inside, where at least half a dozen men were standing around a small fire set in the bottom of a large steel barrel, their faces lit by the faint glow. None of them even slightly resembled Billy Hobbs.

The moment Lyons stepped through the opening, the men around the barrel looked his way, half of them in annoyance, the others with apprehension.

"Hey, man," one of them called out, eyeing Lyons from head to toe, "you're on the wrong side of the tracks."

"Maybe he wants to rob us," another said, laughing. "Damn, and just after that million dollars I won at the Golden Nugget."

"Or maybe he wants to rent a room," a third transient ventured. He looked at Lyons and gestured around at the bleak surroundings. "Got a few vacancies still. How about the presidential suite? You'll love our buffet."

"I'm looking for someone," Lyons said.

"Unless his name's trouble, you've come to the wrong place."

One by one, Boulam, Schwarz and Blancanales appeared elsewhere in the building, surrounding the transients and putting an end to their wisecracking. Lyons gave the squatters a description of Billy Hobbs, adding, "And he just walked out of the hospital, so he's probably pretty weak."

"Yeah, he was here, all right," one of the men admitted.

"Was?" Blancanales said.

The man nodded. "Left here about half an hour ago. I followed him, tried to get him to stay. Like you say, he didn't look so hot. But he wouldn't have any of it. Said he had some business to attend to."

"Where was he going?" Schwarz asked.

The transient shrugged. "Gee, I can't seem to remember."

Lyons reached for his wallet and pulled out a five dollar bill. He handed it to the man. "Here, rub this against your brain and see if your memory comes back"

The transient followed Lyons's advice and smiled. "Hey, whaddya know? It works."

HALF A BLOCK from the Global Imports warehouse, Billy Hobbs paused to catch his breath inside the darkened side doorway of a print shop closed for the evening. The walk from the packing plant, though less than a few hundred yards, had been an ordeal. The mere impact of his footsteps was jarring to his shoulder wound, several times increasing the pain to a point where the youth had been on the verge of collapse. In each case, however, he'd stopped and concentrated on fighting off the blackouts until they passed.

Billy had no idea what he planned to do once he reached the warehouse. He only knew that all his problems of the past few days had stemmed from what had happened there, and by returning to the scene he hoped that somehow he would find a way to make things right. Perhaps deep in the recesses of his feverish brain, recollections from all the pulp detective novels he'd read in prison were giving rise to the notion that if he were to sniff about for clues he would inevitably strike upon a trail that would lead him to those responsible for his dilemma.

Billy was still in the doorway when he heard the dull putter of a small engine, sounding closer by the second. Retreating farther into the darkness, he held his breath as he saw a three-wheeled security vehicle roll past, then idle to a stop less than ten yards from where he was hiding. For several agonizing seconds, Billy felt certain that he'd been discovered and that the uniformed guard inside the vehicle would step out and arrest him, thwarting his quest.

However, it turned out that the guard had merely driven to this remote area of the industrial park for a little privacy as he enjoyed a late-night snack of coffee and doughnuts. While he ate, the guard climbed out of the vehicle and turned up the volume of a radio propped on the dashboard so he could hear the University of Las Vegas basketball game while he skimmed the evening paper in the glow of the headlights.

Seeing the guard's back turned to him, Billy relaxed slightly, at first merely relieved that he hadn't been discovered. As the moment dragged on, however, he became increasingly tempted by the lure of opportunity. From where he was standing, he could see a holstered revolver dangling from the guard's waist. So close, if only...

Slowly, ever so slowly, Billy bent low in the doorway, stretching his hand outward until his fingers closed around a triangular block of wood used to prop the door open during the daytime. Far longer than it was wide, the block fit comfortably in Billy's hand, making a serviceable club. He held it at the ready, and when the game on the radio reached a particularly frenzied point, he took advantage of the loud cheering and crept from the doorway, closing in on the guard.

When Billy's shadow swept across the pavement, the guard glanced up from his newspaper, but by then it was too late to avoid the downthrusting wedge of lumber, which caught him squarely on the back of the head. With a grunt and a thud, the guard tumbled to the ground, unconscious.

The man was too heavy for Billy to move, so he turned off the security vehicle and the radio instead, then crouched beside his victim and undid the snap securing his Smith & Wesson Model 19 to the holster. Slowly withdrawing the weapon, Billy cradled it in his palms. In his teens, his uncle had taught him how to use and respect the power of a handgun, and Billy had proved himself to have a reasonably good aim when they went out to the country to hunt for small game. Now, the feel of the Smith & Wesson filled him with a sense of power and control. He no longer felt so defenseless, so much at the mercy of fate. Now, he felt, it was within his power to seek out retribution for the injustices he'd suffered since the night of the robbery for which he'd been framed.

Rising from his crouch, Billy held the revolver close at his side and circled the print shop. Up ahead lay the Global Imports warehouse, where it had all begun.

Where it would now all end.

22

Parked in front of the Global Imports warehouse, Clint Dirry drummed his fingers nervously on the dashboard of his Jaguar. The dash clock read 10:03 and still none of the others had shown up. He took out his frustration on his cigar, tugging in one last long draw of pungent smoke and blowing it out in one equally long, furious cloud, like a storm god on an old weather map.

What was the plan? he wondered, coming back to the same nagging question that had plagued him since his conversation with Burlington, Alper and Calno back at the Potosi. They had refrained from giving him any details, on the supposed theory that the less he knew, the less he would feel compelled to hide as he set the trap. Now, sitting in his Jaguar with the moment of truth inexplicably delayed, his jangled nerves filled him with doubts.

Could it be that they'd left him in the dark because they planned to double-cross him as well as the others? Would he find himself in police custody and closeted in some interrogation room, trying to vindicate himself in the eyes of his questioners? Or, worse yet, would he join the likes of countless victims who'd been caught up in internecine Mob struggles over the years, slain and taken off the playing board like some expendable pawns in a chess match? As the seconds dragged by, the latter scenario became increasingly vivid in Dirry's mind, and with perverse fascination he began to imagine what it would be like to be murdered. How would that bullet feel piercing his flesh, obliterating brain or heart? Would he indeed be treated to that concentrated flood of memories playing out his whole life before his eyes in the split second it took for his pulse to cease? Or perhaps he would be denied the grace of a quick death and instead be hauled off for torture? Electric prods to the groin, bones shattered by blows with lead pipes, needles jammed beneath the fingernails, well-placed cuts with a razor...he'd heard of a thousand different atrocities a man could be subjected to, sometimes in the hopes of loosening a stubborn tongue, other times merely to provide amusement and a pathetic source of pleasure for the torturer.

"Fuck it," he muttered to himself as the digital clock counted off another minute. He'd done his part. It wasn't his fault that no one had shown up. Why sit around waiting for the shit to hit the fan? They think they have all the answers, let them handle it.

He reached around the steering wheel and was about to start the engine when headlights washed across the Jaguar and another car pulled up in front of the building. Janice Kennesey, behind the wheel of her BMW. She'd picked up Rick Fries on the way over. Fries got out of the passenger's side and circled around to get the door for Janice, but she was already letting herself out. Dirry left his Jaguar and joined them on the sidewalk.

"You're late," he said. "Where's Ned?"

"He said he'd be here." Janice shrugged. "You alone, Clint?"

"Yeah, why?"

"I don't know," Kennesey said. "From the way you were talking, I assumed there'd be some other input."

"There will be down the line," Dirry explained, "but I don't need help spelling things out."

"Maybe we should wait out here for Farrow," Fries suggested, glancing up and down the isolated street. There were only a few untended cars parked along the block and no pedestrians. Several buildings away a steam press hissed and thumped in a steady rhythm.

Janice unlocked the front door the the warehouse. "Ned's got a key. Besides, there are a couple of things I want to check on in the office before we get into this."

The threesome entered the building's small lobby, which was partially lit but empty. With Kennesey leading the way, they walked past a small reception area and through a door behind the service counter to a back hallway. Halfway down the corridor, Janice motioned for them to stop as she inserted a key into a door.

"Just give me a second," she said, starting to open the door. "I have to get a file from—"

To the woman's astonishment, the doorknob slipped out of her hand as the door swung sharply inward, as if of its own accord. She glanced up and found herself staring down the bore of a Walther PPK pistol in the right hand of a man whose face was hidden behind a canary-yellow ski mask.

"What on earth—"

"Silence!" the masked figure hissed in a hoarse, strained whisper obviously intended to disguise his voice.

Kennesey took a step back from the doorway, giving the intruder room to join her and the others in the hallway.

"What's going on here?" Fries demanded, turning to Dirry. "You set us up, you bastard!"

"I don't know anything about this!" Dirry gasped, instinctively throwing his arms in the air when the Walther was aimed his way.

Down the corridor, the door to the main warehouse opened and a second man appeared, wearing a scarlet ski mask and carrying an Uzi submachine gun. He gestured for the group to come his way, and with additional prodding by the other gunman, the three captives began moving.

As she walked, Kennesey gradually overcame her shock, and when they reached the doorway, she calmly addressed the red-masked gunman with the Uzi. "The disguises really aren't necessary, Ralph. Give us credit for a little intelligence, would you?"

"I'm not Ralph." Calno sniggered as he held the door open and motioned for the others to pass through. "I'm Joe Blow, member of ARC."

"Hey, it *is* Ralph!" Fries said, recognizing the man's voice. "What's this ARC shit? Come on, Calno, what's going on?" He looked over his shoulder at the other gunman. "Alper, is that you?"

"Get in the warehouse," the policeman shouted through his yellow mask, waving his Walther for emphasis. "Now!"

In a lower but no less menacing voice Calno quickly added, "And if any of you mention us by name again, it's the last talking you'll ever do. Understood?"

When Fries hesitated, Calno suddenly lashed out with the butt of his Uzi, slamming it into the casino manager's ribs. Doubling over with a groan of pain, Fries reluctantly staggered through the doorway, followed by Kennesey and Dirry. Alper and Calno brought up the rear, closing the door behind them. The warehouse lights were already on, illuminating long, high rows of shelves filled with various import goods packed in cardboard boxes and wooden crates. On the floor in the center of the room, two workers and a security guard lay unconscious, gagged and with their feet bound at the ankles and their hands tied behind their backs.

"You see," Calno explained to the most recent prisoners as he pointed out the fallen trio, "as far as they're concerned, they were jumped by some ARC hotheads looking to make a big move now that the Simms twins have been taken out of the picture."

Alper went over to one of the nearby shelves and tipped over a cardboard box, then pried the top off so he could pull out a thick stack of handbills filled with ARC propaganda. He threw the stack in the air and smiled through his mask as the fliers separated and floated in a zigzag motion to the floor. He spelled out some more of the frame-up. "They decided to cut their losses as far as dealing with the Mob went, but you people weren't that anxious to let them off the hook. There was a struggle," he said, cradling the Walther in both hands and taking aim at Rich Fries. "Shots were fired."

"No, don't!" Fries pleaded. "Come on, let's discuss this!"

"There's nothing to discuss," Calno said, leveling his Uzi at the trio.

"What about me?" Dirry said. "You said that when I got them here I'd be—"

"So we lied," Alper interjected. "Sorry, Clint ol' bean, but you're one chef too many for the new soup, y'know? Tough break, but that's life in the big city."

Janice retained her calm and crossed her arms in front of her, flashing a cool smile. Looking around the warehouse, she said, "So I assume you've planted enough clues around here that no trails are going to lead to you two or to Burlington once the law shows up."

"Yes," Alper boasted. "As far as they're concerned, all the crap going down around town lately has been the result of you three trying to cozy up to ARC for a little extra muscle in expanding your turf. We'll drop them a few hints that you were out to discredit Bobby Sumur by going after his witnesses, too."

"Nice tidy little package," Calno said. "And no need to have the taxpayers pay for a trial, because all the principals are dead."

"Okay," Alper told him. "Enough chitchat. Say your prayers, kids."

The two masked men were preparing to execute Kennesey, Fries and Dirry when a gunshot thundered from across the room and Calno dropped his Uzi in mute surprise as a bullet ripped through his throat.

Blood geysered from the severed carotid artery, soaking the already red material of his mask. The hit man toppled sideways off a stack of wooden skids before striking the ground with a dull thud.

Alper lunged quickly to his right, seeking cover behind a forklift as he traced the trajectory of the shot back to the rear entrance of the warehouse, where Billy Hobbs peered over the top of a huge wooden crate, Smith & Wesson in hand. Caught between the two gunmen, Kennesy, Dirry and Fries dropped to the floor, seeking what refuge they could among the smaller packing boxes.

Billy squeezed off another shot, raising sparks off the surface of the forklift and forcing Alper to duck lower for cover. "Who framed me?" he shouted loudly. His strident voice echoed off the walls of the cavernous enclosure. "Who framed me?"

Fries recognized Hobbs and thought fast. "The other guy with a mask!" he called out. "Get him, too!"

"Bullshit," Alper shouted. He leaned out long enough to fire in Fries's direction, hitting the casino manager in the upper arm before being driven back by another blast from Billy Hobbs's stolen revolver. Fries moaned in pain, rolling on the floor.

"It's true," Janice Kennesey told Billy once she'd safely wriggled below a packing bench that put her out of view of either gunman. "That security guy they killed was going to blow the whistle, so they got rid of him and set you up for the murder. Alper was supposed to shoot you and say you were trying to resist arrest, but you got away."

"This is *her* warehouse," Alper countered. "She's the one you want, not me."

"You're all guilty!" Billy screamed, wasting another shot on the forklift. Delirious with pain and fatigue, he prepared to break from cover. "You'll all pay!"

"Guess again, punk," Ned Farrow said, stepping into view five feet behind the youth and aiming the .454 Casull at his head. Unscrupulous by nature, Farrow nonetheless wasn't one to shoot someone from behind, so he waited for Billy to turn around. That moment of hesitation, however slight, was sufficient for Frank Boulam and Gadgets Schwarz to make their moves. Bursting through the same doorway Calno and Alper had used to bring their prisoners into the warehouse, the two men quickly took firing stances. Billy Hobbs was standing in Schwarz's way, so it was left to Boulam to shoot at Farrow, who turned to face the young Fed.

In some ways, the faceoff was like the duels of the Old West, when gunslingers drew on one another in the middle of Main Street. The main difference, however, was that there had been little buildup and no pregnant pause during which the opponents could stare each other in the eye as if using telepathy to recount the circumstances that had led to their confrontation. In this case, it was two strangers who came up against each other while both were in motion. Farrow was by far the more experienced at such encounters, and his Casull howled first and most accurately. Even as Frank Boulam was pulling his trigger, he was dying from the murderous path a .454 slug had drilled through his chest. His shot flew wild, shattering the exit sign above Farrow's head as the bounty hunter bolted for the doorway through which both he and Billy Hobbs had entered the warehouse. Hobbs fired his Smith & Wesson at the bearded man but his shot missed as well.

Sergeant Alper's thoughts were also on flight, and when he saw that there was a side exit behind him, he scrambled for it, pausing only long enough to turn and distract Schwarz with a stray shot from his Walther. Gadgets was crouched over the inert body of Frank Boulam and easily ducked the bullet. As Alper slipped through the doorway, Schwarz took a quick glance at the fallen federal agent and felt a piercing sadness as he realized the man who had been so honored to be working alongside Able Team had paid the ultimate price for that "honor."

"Bastards," Schwarz muttered at Farrow, at Alper, at all the forces of evil responsible for killing men and women in the line of duty.

ENTERING A LONG CORRIDOR bathed in the fluorescent glow of overhead lights, Alper broke into a full run, yanking the ski mask from his head and discarding it on the linoleum floor. He was twenty yards from the end of the corridor and the hopeful promise of the exit doorway when Carl Lyons suddenly appeared from around the corner ahead of him.

"Oh, you're just in time!" Alper gasped, slowing down and greeting Lyons as an ally. "I just got here and it looks like—"

"Save the acting for the prison play, Alper," Lyons interrupted, pointing his .45 at the sergeant. "And drop that Walther or I'll drop you."

"What?" Alper feigned surprise. "Are you crazy?"

"Shut up and drop the gun!" Lyons commanded. When Alper warily obliged, Ironman strode forward and forced the officer into a spread-eagled position against the wall, telling him, "I've worn a badge, Alper, and let me tell you, there's nothing lower than a cop gone bad."

NED FARROW RACED across the parking lot and was about to climb into his rental car when Pol Blancanales suddenly leaped out at him, seemingly out of nowhere. Farrow lost his grip on his Casull and both men went down to the asphalt in a swirl of flying limbs. Life as a bounty hunter required more than just a good aim, and despite his bulk Farrow was surprisingly nimble and well-versed in the martial arts. Though Blancanales had benefited from the element of surprise, his recent injuries blunted the effectiveness of his assault and Farrow's less-hampered reflexes saved him from being immediately overpowered. He even managed to use the leverage of his powerful legs to shove Blancanales off him several seconds into their struggle, and when Pol slammed backward into the car, absorbing most of the impact with his wounded shoulder, he crumpled over in pain.

Farrow rolled quickly to his right, extending his hand for the Casull, which lay on the asphalt several feet away. Before he could reach it, however, a figure strode into view and kicked the weapon under the car. Farrow glanced up and saw Billy Hobbs staring down at him, aiming the Smith & Wesson at a point between his eyes.

"Billy, don't!" Blancanales cried out, but his voice was smothered by the sound of gunfire.

EPILOGUE

"...I now pronounce you husband and wife," the minister intoned. Turning to Vincent Hobbs, he concluded, "You may kiss the bride."

Shifting on his crutches, Vincent took Bari into his embrace and they kissed to the light applause of the wedding party. Best man Billy Hobbs grinned sheepishly behind his uncle, and in the background Able Team looked on with genuine pleasure at their friend's happiness. Having just attended funeral services for Frank Boulam, they were all in need of the upbeat focus Vinnie's belated wedding provided. Standing with the bridesmaids was Donna Alvarez, weeping both with joy over the occasion and with fond, bittersweet memories of her own wedding. As she dabbed at her tears she caught Pol watching her and offered a slight smile.

Instead of the glitzy, extravagant bash that had originally been planned, the couple had instead chosen the tackier surroundings of the chapel at the Dromedary Hotel, one of the countless dozens of quickie-marriage emporiums Las Vegas was so well-known for. Because three other couples were lined up and waiting for their own ceremonies, the Hobbs party quickly exited the chapel and began piling into cars for the short drive to the outskirts of town, where Vincent's fellow newspaper workers were readying a backyard barbecue reception at the city editor's five-acre home. The newlyweds drove off by themselves while Billy rode with Able Team and Donna Alvarez. A return visit to the hospital and a few days of rest had done wonders for the youth, both physically and mentally.

"I can't thank you guys enough," he told the others. "By rights I should be back behind bars for what I did to Ned Farrow."

"Well, going through the hassle of a trial and playing the temporary insanity game didn't seem like it was going to do anyone any good," Lyons said as he drove across town. "In our book, justice was served. That's what's important. That and the fact that you've promised to keep your nose clean."

"I'm sure going to try," Billy said. He turned to Donna. "Getting that job at the rescue mission will help. A lot."

"You'll be a welcome addition there, I'm sure," Donna told him.

Although they were driving several streets away from the Strip, the larger casinos were still visible in the distance. Spotting the glowing lights of the Caravan, Billy asked Able Team, "Were you able to nab everyone in that whole mob?"

"We made a pretty good sweep, I think," Schwarz said, "but with those people there's no such thing as 'nabbing everyone.' We know for sure that a guy named Burlington's still on the loose, probably back east by now, and some other players will lie low for a while, then turn up again. Same with ARC. It'd be nice to think we were rid of them once and for all, but we know better.''

"Doesn't it get frustrating?'' Billy wondered. "I mean, it seems like no matter how much you do or how many scumbags you take off the street, there's always going to be more crawling out of the sewers to take their place.''

"Well put, Billy,'' Schwarz said. "And, yeah, it sure as hell gets frustrating, especially when good men like Frank Boulam go down in the fight. But look at it this way, if we weren't out there at least putting a dent in things, imagine how much worse it would be.''

"How about if we don't discuss this for the next few hours?'' Donna suggested from the back seat. "We're celebrating a wedding, so the least we can do is try to be cheerful about it, don't you think?''

"Absolutely,'' Pol said. "Hey, Ironman, how about we swing by Pedro's and get a few orders of fried rice to throw at the lucky couple.''

From Europe to Africa, the Executioner stalks his elusive enemy—a cartel of ruthless men who might prove too powerful to defeat.

DON PENDLETON's

MACK BOLAN

Moving Target

One of America's most powerful corporations is reaping huge profits by dealing in arms with anyone who can pay the price. Dogged by assassins, Mack Bolan follows his only lead fast and hard—and becomes caught up in a power struggle that might be his last.

Available now at your favorite retail outlet, or reserve your copy for shipping by sending your name, address, zip or postal code along with a check or money order for $4.70 (includes 75¢ for postage and handling) payable to Gold Eagle Books to:

In the U.S.

Gold Eagle Books
901 Fuhrmann Blvd.
Box 1325
Buffalo, NY 14269-1325

In Canada

Gold Eagle Books
P.O. Box 609
Fort Erie, Ontario
L2A 5X3

Please specify book title with your order.

SB-14A

A stark account of one of the Vietnam War's most controversial
defense actions.

VIETNAM: GROUND ZERO™

Shifting
FIRES

ERIC HELM

For seventy-seven days and nights six thousand Marines held the
remote plateau of Khe Sanh without adequate supplies or ammunition. As General Giap's twenty thousand troops move in to
bring the NVA one step closer to victory, an American Special
Forces squad makes a perilous jump into the mountainous Khe
Sanh territory in a desperate attempt to locate and destroy Giap's
command station.

**Phoenix Force—bonded in secrecy to avenge the acts
of terrorists everywhere.**

Super Phoenix Force #2

American "killer" mercenaries are involved in a KGB plot to
overthrow the government of a South Pacific island. The American President, anxious to preserve his country's image and not
disturb the precarious position of the island nation's government, sends in the experts—Phoenix Force—to prevent a coup.

You don't know what NONSTOP HIGH-VOLTAGE ACTION Is until you've read your 4 FREE GOLD EAGLE NOVELS